IN MEMORY OF
Gorfman T. Frog

In Memory of

Gorfman T. Frog

Gail Donovan

SCHOLASTIC INC.
New York Toronto London Auckland
Sydney Mexico City New Delhi Hong Kong

ISBN 978-0-545-24232-5

Text copyright © 2009 by Gail Donovan.
Illustrations copyright © 2009 by Janet Pedersen.
All rights reserved. Published by Scholastic Inc.,
557 Broadway, New York, NY 10012, by arrangement with
Dutton Children's Books, a division of Penguin Young Readers Group,
a member of Penguin Group (USA) Inc. SCHOLASTIC and associated
logos are trademarks and/or registered trademarks of Scholastic Inc.

12 11 10 9 8   12 13 14 15/0

Printed in the U.S.A.   40

First Scholastic printing, March 2010

Designed by Irene Vandervoort

For Zora, who inspired this book,

and Lydia-Rose,

who named it

—G.D.

Acknowledgments

My thanks to Ann Harleman,
Elizabeth Searle, and Frances Lefkowitz.

Contents:

Chapter 1

Josh Explodes

The alarm went off like it wanted to do permanent damage to Josh's brain. Time to get up. If his legs still worked after last night's practice. *Run! Run! Run! Let's see some legs out there!*

Josh got out of bed, which he considered a minor miracle, trudged downstairs, and opened the fridge, still trying to wake up. The cold air helped. It was going to be another hot, sticky day. Thursday. Two days to go until the game. Last Saturday he'd gotten a hit. *Thwack*—he made contact. *Zoom*—the ball went flying. *Yes*—a solid single.

"It's a hit!" he boomed. "Hewitt is on base! Let's hear it for Joshua Tree Hewitt!"

Josh was named for a place his mom claimed was so beautiful—Joshua Tree National Park. Josh had seen pictures. The spiky-leaved trees looked like something out of Dr. Seuss. But if he was going to be named for a park, why couldn't it have been something cool, like *Death Valley*?

"What are you talking about?" asked Cady. She was sitting at the kitchen table, eating toast and reading. On the cover of her book was a horse with a tail and mane the exact shade of brown as Cady's ponytail, which came down to her waist.

Cady's real name was Acadia, which was another park their mom really liked. She was seven and in second grade, and when she wasn't reading horse books she was playing with toy horses. Or trotting around and jumping imaginary jumps, like she *was* a horse.

"My hit," said Josh. "The one I made last weekend, remember?"

"Get over it," said Cady. She stood and, lifting up her hands into the rein-holding position, started to trot from the room.

"Hey!" said Josh. "I don't get it. It's like you have people-hands and horse-legs. So which are you? The horse or the rider?"

"Both," said Cady, and trotted off.

4

"Whatever," said Josh, peering into the open fridge. Orange juice, cream, beer. Where was the milk?

"Milk!" shouted Josh. "Let's see some legs! Run! Run! Run!"

"No more running," panted Josh's mom, coming into the kitchen. "I just did six miles."

Josh's mom ran every day. She said if she didn't get her run in, she'd bite somebody's head off. Then, as if jogging every morning wasn't enough, she spent the rest of the day jumping around with a bunch of other women at the fitness studio she ran. Sometimes she called Josh motormouth, but he thought it was like she was a motorbody.

His mom reached into the open fridge for the orange juice, poured a glass, then took a long swig. Then she stared at Josh as if she was seeing him for the first time. Slowly, she asked, "What. Are. You. *Doing*?"

"Looking. For. The. Milk," Josh answered back. He liked the way he sounded, sort of like a robot, so he kept going. "But. I. Don't. See. Any."

Josh's mom held up her hand. "We're out of milk," she said. "And you know what I meant. What's the rule?"

Josh knew the rule, but if she wanted him to recite it like some kind of parrot, that was fine with him. "Clothes first, then breakfast," he said, and made a noise like a parrot squawk. "Breakfast in pajamas is for weekends. Unless I have an early game." He squawked again. "That's the rule."

"If you know the rule," she said, "then why are you breaking it?"

"Mom," said Josh. "I didn't wake up and think, Let's go break a rule! I just woke up hungry. And I don't see what difference it makes if I get dressed first and then eat, or eat first and then get dressed. I mean, I have to do both before I go to school, right?"

Smiling, Josh's mom shook her head. "Serves me right for asking you a question. Never mind. You need to stop talking and start getting ready for school. And stop standing there with the fridge wide open!"

"I'm *trying* to get ready for school, but there's no milk," he said, and added, "Payson doesn't have to get dressed to eat breakfast, and plus his mom buys frozen waffles. I don't see why you can't buy frozen waffles, or they have frozen pancakes, too—"

"Josh!" said his mother. "When you're talking, you're not moving. So close your mouth, please. And please close the refrigerator."

Josh hated it when grown-ups said *please* when they weren't really asking. They were giving you an order. Okay: order given; order received. He pushed the fridge closed so hard that the bottles on the inside of the door rattled.

"Joshua," said his mother. "Please don't slam doors!"

Josh's dad came into the kitchen. "What's up?" he asked, supercalm.

That was the thing about Josh's dad: he was good at staying calm in an emergency. He had to be. He worked in the emergency room at the hospital. He was so good at staying calm, Josh sometimes wondered if he even knew how to get upset.

Josh's mom said, "*Somebody's* going to miss the bus again."

Josh's dad said, "You'll make it if you start hustling. Get some breakfast, okay?"

Josh pulled a box of cereal from the cupboard. "I'm *trying* to," he said. "But there's no milk."

"Don't argue," said his father. "Just do it."

Cady came trotting back into the kitchen. "Hey!" she said. "How come he gets to eat breakfast in his pajamas!"

It was bad enough that his sister was practically perfect in his parents' eyes. Did she have to point out his flaws, too?

"'Cause I'm so special," he said.

"Mom!" protested Cady.

Josh's dad said, "Take it easy, Cady. And Josh, Cady wasn't talking to you, so you didn't really need to say that, did you? I want you to start pretending you've got a remote control. It has a pause button. Use it. Just pause before you say every single thing that comes into your head, okay?"

"Why don't you just tell me to shut up?" shouted Josh. "That's what you mean!"

Josh's mom answered, "Because we don't use that sort of language around here. Come on, Josh. You know better than that."

"Fine," said Josh. "I get the concept. Pause button." He pointed an imaginary remote at himself and pushed an imaginary button. Then he opened up the china cabinet, took out a bowl, and shook in some cereal.

Cady said, "If he misses the bus, can I get a ride to school, too?"

"Nobody is missing the bus," said Josh's mom. "And Josh, would you please close the cabinet after you open it?"

He couldn't do anything right! They wanted the cabinet closed? Fine! He took the handle and slammed it as hard as he could. Closed!

There was a noise like ice cracking, and Josh stared in surprise as shards of glass rained down on the kitchen floor. He'd meant to close the glass-fronted cabinet door. He'd even meant to slam it. But he didn't mean for it to break.

"Joshua Tree Hewitt," snapped his mom. "I *just* asked you not to slam doors!"

"I didn't!"

"What do you mean?" she cried. "We just saw you slam it!"

Josh tried to explain. "I mean I was trying to close it like you *told* me to, but I wasn't *trying* to break it—"

"Enough!" Josh's mom held up her hand like a crossing guard stopping traffic.

"What is wrong with you?" demanded his father, looking at Josh as if he was some kind of freak. "When you do something wrong, you don't argue. You just say you're sorry."

"I'm not arguing," he protested. "But if you think I was trying to break it, then that's not fair, because I wasn't. I mean, I'm sorry it got broken, but it's not like I *tried* to break it, and you're acting like I did—"

Up went the hand again, and Josh stopped trying to explain. It was hopeless anyway. The more he talked, the more mad they got. As usual.

Except he had one more thing to say: "I said I was sorry!"

"You did," admitted his mom wearily. "Somewhere in there, you did. Now I'm going to clean this up, and you're going to eat breakfast. But tonight we're going to have a serious talk."

"Okay," said Josh's dad. "Let's get rolling, because you are not missing that bus again." He opened up the fridge. "No milk. Right. Well, you can put some water in this cream and it'll be like milk."

"Gross!" said Josh. "No way!"

"It's either that or orange juice in your cereal."

"Fine!" said Josh stubbornly. "I'll have orange juice!"

"Suit yourself." Josh's dad sloshed some juice into the bowl and handed it to Josh. "Now hurry up and eat your"—he grimaced at the cereal floating in the orange liquid—"breakfast."

Josh headed out to the back porch, and as the screen door slammed behind him he heard his dad ask, "What is his *problem*?" Then his mother closed the wooden door so he wouldn't hear the answer.

Josh sat down on the porch steps. He didn't need to hear his parents to know what they were saying the problem was: he talked too much.

He couldn't help it. He talked to himself. He talked to his friends. He even talked to the sunflowers growing beside the back porch.

"Come on, guys," he said. "Power up. Make me proud."

The plants were only knee-high now, but Josh was hoping they were going to be mammoth. Last fall he had saved the seeds from the tallest sunflower he could find, and this spring he had planted them. He was going to save the seeds from whichever plant grew biggest this year to grow even bigger ones next year, and even bigger ones the year after that.

In the meantime, he was supposed to be eating breakfast.

Josh peered doubtfully at the bowl in his hands. Oat pops floating in orange juice. Not a pretty picture. He dipped in his spoon and tried putting a spoonful in his mouth, but even before he swallowed he could feel his stomach sending up a warning: *Alarm! Alarm! Definitely not edible! Eject! Eject!*

He yanked the spoon out of his mouth and tossed it. The spoon landed in the garden pool with a splash. A second later he heard another splash.

Josh tiptoed across the patio flagstones to investigate. There was something in there besides water lilies—something swimming! A frog!

"I'm gonna getcha," he said. He reached for the frog and missed. Now the frog was kicking around in the middle of the pool, out of Josh's reach. Warning the frog, *"You can't escape the long arm of Death Valley!"* he waded into the water.

The screen door slammed.

"Joshua Tree Hewitt," cried his mom, "what are you *doing*?"

"There's a frog," called Josh as he lunged. "And I got it!"

"And I'm going to eat frog legs for supper," she yelled, "if you don't get yourself ready to go, *right now*!"

Josh stood up and almost dropped the frog. Was he seeing clearly?

He could feel his waterlogged pajamas sliding down his behind, but he didn't dare reach to hold them up. There was no way he could risk letting go of *this* frog!

"Uh, Mom," he said, "I don't think you should eat these frog legs."

"And why is that?"

"'Cause he's got one too many."

Chapter 2

Thanks, Frog

Eeew!" shrieked his mom, quickly followed by "Ow!" because she had spilled hot coffee on herself. Finally she got some real words out. "I don't believe this," she said. "I do not believe it. David!"

Josh looked at the frog and the frog looked right back at him with its big frog eyes, like it was saying, *You got a problem with this?* And for a second Josh was thinking, Yes! Of course he had a problem with a five-legged frog!

Then the frog, wriggling, touched one of its feet to Josh's bare arm, straining to get away.

"Hey, that tickles!" said Josh, holding on tight. The frog was green with big black spots, and its skin felt smooth and cool. He could feel its heart thumping.

"David!" called Josh's mom again. "Come see this!"

Josh's dad pushed open the screen door. "Wow," was all he said, totally calm.

Cady came out on the back stoop. "Gross!" she shrieked. "Double gross!"

That settled it. "It is not gross!" said Josh.

"Yes, it is!" cried Cady.

"Well, it probably thinks you're gross!" said Josh. "Did you ever think of that?"

"Mo-om!" complained Cady.

Just then Josh heard the school bus chugging up the hill. He braced himself. First he'd broken the cupboard glass and now he'd missed the bus. Even if his mother had just run six miles, she still might bite off his head.

The bus came into view, first tiny and yellow, then big and yellow, like an out-of-control, mutant sunflower. It slowed down in front of their house, but Josh's father waved it on. "I'll give them a ride," he said.

Saved! Relief washed over Josh. This was one

time calm-in-a-crisis was working in his favor. "Thanks, Dad."

"Don't thank me," said Josh's father. "Thank that frog."

Josh grinned at the frog. "Thanks, frog!"

Josh's mom said, "I guess we can add missing the bus to the list of things to discuss tonight. Now, what are you going to do with that . . . frog?"

"Why don't you bring him in for sharing?" suggested Cady, and, pretending to be Josh, she said in a singsong voice, "'Oh, Ms. O'Reilly, I have something special to share. . . .'"

Josh flashed his sister a grin, and together he and Cady let out a mock scream: "Aaah!"

Half an hour later, Josh was in Hollison Elementary with a bucket in his hand, waiting for the morning announcements to be done. Ms. O'Reilly had said he could share right afterward.

Good morning, came a kid's voice over the intercom. *Today is Thursday, June 1. Hot lunch will be . . .*

Josh stopped listening and started jiggling his leg against the side of the bucket, until he realized that he was probably making the frog seasick. He felt kind of seasick himself. What was Ms. O'Reilly going to say about his frog? He didn't really want to scare her. He wanted her to like it.

Ms. O'Reilly had started out the year liking him because he raised his hand a lot. A raised hand meant you were paying attention. Teachers loved that. Then she decided that his answers were too talky. Long-winded, she said. This was fifth grade, she said, and she wanted straight answers. Honestly, she didn't know what they'd been doing in fourth grade. She'd been teaching for twenty-seven years and she'd never had a class less ready for middle school.

So she'd stopped calling on him so much, and Josh had started going crazy. Sometimes he talked without being called on first. Teachers hated that.

Sometimes he just talked to the kids next to him. She hated that, too.

But hopefully bringing in this frog could fix him up with Ms. O'Reilly. He didn't want the honor of graduating as the worst kid in the worst class of Ms. O'Reilly's twenty-seven-year teaching career.

And Happy Birthday to Aidan Roderick.

The intercom went silent, and Ms. O'Reilly stood up in front of the class.

"All right, fifth graders," she said. "Joshua has brought in something to share with us." Ms. O'Reilly had short gray hair and glasses. Half the time her glasses perched on the tip of her nose and half the time they dangled around her neck from a chain made out of sea glass. She gave Josh a go-ahead smile. "All right, Joshua."

Josh set the bucket on the floor, took off the lid, reached in, and put his hands around the frog's middle. "This," he announced, lifting the frog up in the air so that its three hind legs dangled down, "is my frog."

Kendra screamed. Lisbet and Mariah, who always did everything together, screamed in unison.

Charu stood on her chair—not like she was scared, Josh thought, but to see better.

Ben B. and Ben T. jumped out of their seats and surged forward to get a closer look.

"Let me see!" said Payson.

Payson wasn't tall and he wasn't even that big, but he was *solid*. When he ran down the soccer field, kids got out of his way. He easily pushed through the other fifth graders to the front. "Awesome!"

"Totally awesome," agreed Ben B.

"No!" said Ben T. "Toadly awesome! Get it? *Toadly*?"

Josh was surprised to see Michael, a skinny kid with curly dark hair, stand on a desk for a better view. Michael didn't usually do anything that would draw attention to himself. He was the kind of kid who never raised his hand. Josh didn't know if Michael knew the answers but was shy, or if he just didn't know the answers.

Josh was even more surprised when Michael gave him a thumbs-up sign. He couldn't let go of the frog, so he just grinned back.

"Fifth graders!" said Ms. O'Reilly. "Fifth graders, we do not stand on chairs and desks!" She raised her hand in the air for order. But the class was so excited, she didn't get order. She had to resort to what they did at schoolwide assemblies. She clapped out

a rhythm: *clap, clap, clap-clap-clap.* Then the kids echoed it back: *clap, clap, clap-clap-clap.*

Charu got off her chair and Michael got down from the desk. The other kids took their seats again.

"Where in the world," said Ms. O'Reilly, reaching for her sea-glass chain and putting her glasses on for an up-close look at the frog, "did this come from?"

"My yard," said Josh, grinning. "There's this place in the woods behind our yard that's pretty soggy, with skunk cabbages and everything, and sometimes I find frogs there. I think maybe it hopped from there to this pool—not a swimming pool, but like a little pool with water lilies."

While he talked, Ms. O'Reilly smiled and nodded. She asked the class, "How could this have happened? Any ideas?"

Kendra's hand shot up. Usually she didn't answer questions because she was busy trying to sneak-read books inside her desk. She said, "Maybe it was born like that."

Charu was waving her hand in the air. No surprise there. She was one of those "ooh-ooh-call-on-me" kids. Except unlike Josh, she usually had the sort of answer the teacher was looking for. She was also the best speller in the fifth grade. "It couldn't have been born that way because it isn't born with any legs at all!"

"Yeah!" said Ben T. He and Ben B. shared the same name, but Ben B. had carrot-orange hair, and Ben T. had a chipped front tooth. He said, "Because it starts out as an egg and then it's a tadpole and then it gets legs!"

"Maybe it's like Siamese twins," offered Lisbet. "Maybe a couple of frog eggs got stuck together or something and turned into one frog with too many legs."

"I don't think so," said Josh. He couldn't raise his hand because he was still holding the frog, but Ms. O'Reilly smiled at him to go on. "'Cause then it would have more than one extra thing. Like an extra front leg, or an extra head!"

The mention of an extra head made Lisbet and

Mariah squeal, and Ben B. and Ben T. groan with delight. But even with all the noise, Ms. O'Reilly just beamed at Josh. Taking the lid off the terrarium, she asked, "Why don't you put your frog in here for the day, Joshua? And then, let's see"—she examined her watch—"we're supposed to have Silent Reading now . . . but I'm going to call the library and see if we can go look for any material that will help us learn more about your frog."

"Yes!" cheered Payson.

Payson hated Silent Reading time. It wasn't that he couldn't read well. It was that he hated being quiet, just like Josh. Way back in kindergarten, they used to build things with blocks and talk. Talking in kindergarten was called socialization. It was a good thing. Then in first grade the teacher moved their desks apart so they couldn't talk too much. After that, they got put in separate classes. But this year enrollment was down. There were only enough kids for one fifth grade, so Josh and Payson were in the same class again.

Josh gently lowered his frog into the glass case. "Look, here's some moss. Here's some water. You can spend the whole day here."

Payson came up and tapped on the terrarium. "How you doing, Froggy?"

"Hey," said Josh quickly. "How would you like it if a giant frog started knocking on the window of your house? That's what it's like when you bang on the glass!"

"All right," agreed Payson. "I won't bother the freaky froggy."

Michael came up to the terrarium and, for the second time that morning, surprised Josh. He asked Josh a direct question. "How'd you find him?"

"I was eating breakfast outside," explained Josh, "except it was so gross I threw the spoon in our pond and that made the frog jump, and then I found him."

Payson had stopped tapping the glass, but Josh could still hear him talking to the frog, saying, "Hey, Freaky Froggy, jump!" And he could hear Ms. O'Reilly on the phone with the school librarian: ". . . special opportunity . . . teachable moment . . . books on amphibians."

"Think there's any more?" asked Michael.

"Maybe," answered Josh. "You could come over and we can look."

Michael's eyes opened wide. "Really?"

"Sure," said Josh. His mom had a rule that she had to talk to the parents first, so he said, "I'll get my mom to call your mom."

"Really?" repeated Michael. "I mean—sure!"

Josh realized that he'd gone to school with this kid for years and hardly ever talked to him. But they were talking now, because of the frog.

Ms. O'Reilly was off the phone. "Line up!" she said. "We're going to the library. Joshua, why don't you take the lead?"

Josh went to the head of the line. Payson got behind him and gave him a congratulatory punch in the arm. Behind them came Charu, Lisbet and Mariah, Ben B. and Ben T., Kendra, Michael, and the rest of the fifth grade.

The whole room was buzzing. It felt like Halloween, or the last day of school, only *he* was the reason for all the excitement.

Well, him and the frog.

Josh liked this feeling. He was a star.

Chapter 3

The Serious Talk

Josh lifted up his hamburger bun and squirted a big glob of ketchup onto the meat. He might have been a star in fifth grade, but he didn't expect any star treatment at home. Any minute now, he expected the Serious Talk. Replacing the bun, he picked up his warm, ketchupy burger.

"Cady," said Josh's dad. "Would you say grace, please?"

Josh put down his hamburger. Whenever they asked him to say grace he usually ended up winging it, and when he was done his father would say something like "That wasn't a grace, it was a speech." More often they asked Cady, who had about ten grace-y poems memorized.

"For every cup and plateful," said Cady, "please make us truly grateful."

Josh was glad she'd picked one of the short poems; he was starving. "Amen," he said loudly, and picking up his burger again, he bit into the warm meat.

"Lacey called," said Josh's mom. "She and Matt want you to sleep over on Saturday."

Was that going to be the punishment? That he couldn't go? Josh chewed quickly so he could protest without being told not to talk with his mouth full, but before he could swallow, his mom added, "I knew you'd want to, so I said yes for you, okay?"

"Thanks, Mom!"

Was this his lucky day or what? He'd found an amazing frog *and* he was a star at school *and* he was going to Matt and Lacey's?

Matt and Lacey were his grandparents. Josh had three sets.

Grandma and Grandpa were his mom's mom and dad; they lived in Massachusetts and Josh saw them on holidays like Thanksgiving. Nana and Pop were his dad's mom and dad; they lived up north, almost in Canada, and his dad took him up there in the summer when they went canoeing.

Matt and Lacey were the mom and dad of Jonathan, Josh's first dad. He and Josh's mom had split up when Josh was a baby, and then he'd died in a car accident. Then Josh's mom got married to David, and they had Cady. His mom called Jonathan Josh's biological father and David his forever father. David had adopted Josh, and he was the only dad Josh knew. But he still had this whole other set of relatives left over from his first dad. Like Matt and Lacey. He called them the bio-grands.

Cady said, "If he gets to have a sleepover, can I have one, too?"

"We'll see," said their mother. "Tell us about your day, Cady."

Their parents said that there was more to good table manners than holding your fork correctly. There was pleasant conversation. When your mouth wasn't full.

"It was good," said Cady. She didn't really get the pleasant conversation concept.

Their dad tried Josh. "How did your teacher like the frog?"

Josh sat up on the edge of his chair. "She loved it! We got to go to the library and get out books on amphibians, and I looked up all the Maine species, and I'm pretty sure it's a leopard frog 'cause of the spots. And I think it must be at least a year old and just came out of hibernation, 'cause it's so big, and— no thanks to salad, Mom!"

Josh's mom put some salad onto his plate. "You mean yes please to salad. Where's the frog now?"

"School," said Josh. "In the terrarium."

His father asked, "How does he like it in there?"

"I don't know," admitted Josh. "It seemed like a nice place for him. There's no predators in there. And there's moss and water. But there's nothing for him to eat. The book said they eat insects, so I'm going to catch some and bring them in tomorrow. And they eat small vertebrates like mice, so I was hoping maybe we could go to a pet store and I could buy some with my own money?"

To show what a worthy candidate he was for a special trip to town, Josh speared a big piece of lettuce and swallowed it without grimacing. "Please?"

"That is so mean," said Cady. "The poor mice!"

"But he needs food!" protested Josh. "He looks weak. After I put him in the terrarium he didn't move all day. I think something might be wrong with him."

His father joked, "You mean, something besides having five legs?"

"Dad, that isn't funny!" said Josh. But his parents were both laughing, and so was Cady. Josh set down his hamburger.

"It's not funny!" he repeated.

"Yes, it is," giggled Cady.

"No, it's not!" said Josh. "The frog can't help the way it is! Just because it has too many legs doesn't make him less good as a frog. It doesn't make him a freak."

"Okay, I'm sorry I teased," said Josh's dad. "But seriously, wouldn't you say it was a 'freak of nature'? In the literal sense?"

"I guess so," said Josh grudgingly. "But that doesn't mean Payson has to call it Freaky Froggy!"

Cady giggled again. "Freaky Froggy?"

"Don't say that!" said Josh.

"Josh!" said his mother. "You don't need to shout."

While their mom wasn't looking, Cady silently mouthed, "Freaky Froggy!"

"Shut up!" roared Josh, lunging for Cady across the table.

Josh's dad reached out and wrapped his big hand around Josh's arm to stop him, and his mom said, "Joshua Tree Hewitt, there will be no fighting at the dinner table."

"That is so unfair," protested Josh. "How come it's always my fault if me and Cady have a fight?"

"You started it," said Cady.

"*You* did," said Josh, "but you're such a goody-goody suck-up they don't even see it—"

"Enough!" snapped his mom, holding up her crossing guard hand. "Cady, you're excused."

"What about dessert?" asked Cady.

"No dessert," said their mom.

Cady made a face, but she put her plate in the sink, picked up her reins, and left the room at a slow trot.

"Remember that pause button we talked about?" asked his dad. "That would have been a good time to push it. About a minute ago."

"All right," said his mom. "Let's go back to this morning. You broke a cabinet, and you missed the bus again. How did that happen?"

What could he possibly say that would make them happy? Nothing he said was ever right. "I found a frog with five legs?"

His dad said, "You found the frog *after* you broke the cabinet, Josh."

"Yeah," said Josh, "but I bet I wouldn't have missed the bus if I hadn't found the frog. And I wouldn't have found the frog if I wasn't eating breakfast outside. And I wouldn't have been eating breakfast outside if I hadn't broken the cabinet. Which I'm not saying was a good thing or anything, but you've got to admit the frog is pretty amazing."

Josh's mom put her elbows on the table and rested her head in her hands, like this conversation was making her tired. "You're going at this completely backwards. We didn't ask how you found the frog. We asked how you could get so worked up that you broke a cabinet."

Josh couldn't resist this opportunity. "My super-power strength?"

His dad said, "This isn't a joke, Joshua!"

"Sorry," said Josh quickly. "But I don't know how it happened. It just . . . happened. I was trying to explain to Mom and she kept getting mad and not letting me explain . . . and then I was just trying to close the cabinet, and . . ." He shrugged. "I don't *know*."

"Josh," said his mom, "I need to be able to tell you to stop talking without you flying into a rage."

"I didn't fly into a rage," echoed Josh. "I just got mad because you were mad at me first. It's like you're always mad at me."

"How can you say that?" she asked. "I'm not always mad at you."

His dad made a referee's T-shape with his hands. "Time out," he said. "Let's try something besides talking. Here's what I propose. You're going to write a short essay about what went wrong this morning, and how to make sure it doesn't happen again."

"Right now?"

His dad pushed a piece of paper and a pen in front of Josh. "Right now."

"That's my punishment?" asked Josh. "I thought it'd be like no computer for a week."

"Good idea," said his mom. "Since you mentioned it, that will be your punishment. This will be your community service."

"But, Mom, I need to go online to learn more about the frog! There's nothing in the library books about this!"

Josh's dad said, "What you need to learn is that every time you open your mouth, you make it worse." He picked up the pen and handed it to Josh.

Josh took the pen. If this wasn't the real punishment, he might as well write whatever he wanted.

You expect me to follow the rules. These are the rules. 1) Come down dressed for breakfast. 2) Quick response! That means if you ask me to do something, I should do it quick. 3) First obey, then talk. That means if I disagree with what you want me to do, I should do it anyway, and we can talk about it later. If I follow all the rules, I won't miss the bus. And we will all live happily ever after. Including the frog. The end.

Josh handed the paper to his parents and waited for them to read it. The house was so quiet that through the screen door he could hear the sound of the spring peepers trilling. He remembered that he wanted to ask his mom to call Michael Robinson's mom. He knew better than to ask right now, though. You had to time your requests to increase the chance of a yes, and this was definitely not the right time. Not yet.

His parents looked at each other the way they did when they were trying to come to a quick decision in front of the kids.

Then they both burst out laughing. They liked it!

Josh decided this was the right time to ask: "Can Michael Robinson come over tomorrow? He wants to see where the frog came from. So will you call his mom?"

His mom said, "Sure," and she went to get the school directory.

Cady must have decided that this was also the

right moment for a request. She stuck her head through the doorway. "Can we have cookies?"

"Sure," said Josh's dad. "Cookies all around."

Cady got out a box of chocolate chip cookies.

Talking on the phone, Josh's mom gave him a thumbs-up that meant Mrs. Robinson was saying yes. "So they can ride the bus here . . . not a problem, we can bring him home later . . ." She said good-bye, hung up, and took a cookie. "All set."

"Thanks, Mom." Josh bit into a cookie.

It had been a crazy day. He'd found a frog with five legs. He'd gotten back in good with his teacher. He'd gotten in trouble with his parents and then, basically, out of trouble. And he'd made friends with Michael Robinson, and tomorrow Michael was coming over after school. All in all, way more good stuff than bad.

Chapter 4

Severe Consequences

Josh bounded off the bus, ran up the stairs into the classroom, and hurried over to the terrarium. He drew a plastic bag from his backpack and pulled out three moths he'd caught on the porch light.

"Breakfast," he announced, dropping the moths into the tank. "Come and get it!"

The frog didn't come and get the moths. The frog didn't look so good. Its black spots looked sort of . . . gray. Josh started trying to count them. One, two, three . . . He was up to twelve when Charu with her long braid came over.

"What are you doing," she interrupted, "studying for the quiz?"

"Quiz!" hissed Payson. "What quiz?"

"*Math*?" she said in a mocking voice. "The quiz we have every Friday?"

Josh hadn't studied, but he wasn't worried about the quiz. He did okay in math. Besides, he had more important things to worry about. His frog. "Eat," he said. "Come on, just one little bite."

Good morning, came a voice over the intercom. *Today is Friday, June 2.*

"Hey!" said Charu. "It's Lisbet!"

"Good," said Josh.

The upper grades took turns making the morning announcements. If Lisbet was announcing, that meant other students in Ms. O'Reilly's class would get a chance soon. Josh hoped his turn came before school let out for summer.

Payson poked Josh. "Did you study?"

Hot lunch today is taco boats and fruit cup.

"No." Josh shook his head. "Do you think the frog looks sick? Maybe I should take it to a vet. You think there are vets for amphibians? I bet a vet would look at a turtle, right? So maybe one would look at a frog."

"Maybe," said Payson.

"Don't you even care?" asked Josh.

When the school had first separated him and Payson, they'd still played together at recess. But it wasn't the same as having your buddy in your class. So when Josh found out that he and Payson were going to be in fifth grade together, he had figured they'd be instant best friends again.

Happy Birthday to Kolby Tinkham!

But Payson hadn't acted like a friend this year. Mostly he ignored Josh and hung out with the two Bens. Then yesterday he had banged on the frog's tank. Today he was back to ignoring him.

Josh repeated, "Don't you even care about the frog?"

"Sure I do," said Payson. "But my mom says I can't play baseball if my math grades get any lower. She says I might have to go to some math-tutoring place after school instead of practice!"

"She can't do that! You're like the best kid on the team!"

"She can if she wants to," said Payson glumly.

"Quick!" said Josh. "Go practice multiplying or something!"

"It's hopeless," said Payson, but he went to his desk and started rummaging around for his math notebook.

Josh turned back to his frog. "Eat," he pleaded. "You can do it. I know you can."

Through the glass tank Josh saw Michael come into the classroom with Mariah and Lisbet. Michael made a beeline for the terrarium.

"How's the frog?" he asked. "Hey, it looks like he hasn't moved!"

"I know," said Josh.

"All right, fifth graders, listen up!" Ms. O'Reilly slipped her glasses off her nose and let them dangle from the chain made of sea glass. "I'm depending on all of you to be cooperators this morning, because we're going to do something very special. We are going outside."

For a second the noisy class was stunned into silence. Ms. O'Reilly hardly ever took them outdoors. Too much opportunity for chaos.

Charu's hand shot up in the air.

"Yes, Charu?"

"What about the math quiz?"

"No quiz today," announced Ms. O'Reilly. "In order to learn more about Joshua's frog, we're going to do a special activity on the food chain."

Charu put her arm down, looking pouty, but everyone else looked thrilled. Kendra closed the book she had open inside her desk. Payson shouted "Yes!" and pounded Josh in the arm. No math quiz meant no danger of not playing baseball.

Normally Josh would have been as excited as everyone else to go outside instead of taking a math quiz. But not this time. His frog needed help. He raised his arm—which was getting sore from all of Payson's congratulatory punches—and said, "Ms. O'Reilly! Ms. O'Reilly!"

"Not now, Joshua," said Ms. O'Reilly. "I'll answer questions when we get outside." Her eyebrows were arched in expectation. "Lead the way, please!"

One teacher was giving him the evil eye, and seventeen kids were jostling and pushing, waiting for Josh to go.

So Josh went.

He marched down the second-floor corridor, past the rooms of the fourth graders, then the third graders, who all peered out of their doorways to see what was happening, then down the stairs, along the first-floor hallway, past the kindergartners' construction-paper tulips and daffodils and *things that come up in the spring!"*

Josh pushed open the big double doors to the playground. A warm breeze made it feel more like summer than spring. It should be against the law to keep kids in school when the weather was this nice. Worst of all, they'd had so many snow days this winter that they were trapped here until the end of June.

"Listen up!" called Ms. O'Reilly. "We're going to play a game that explores the food chain. You will each have a role to play in our make-believe food chain. I'm going to assign your roles now, so pay attention."

Payson, Michael, and Kendra were frogs. Everybody else was a grasshopper, except Josh. He was a hawk.

"He's an apex predator!" shouted Payson. "Right at the top of the food chain!"

Everybody laughed, except Josh. He couldn't stop thinking about his frog, locked up in a glass box. He tried raising his hand again. "Ms. O'Reilly?"

"Not now, Josh," said Ms. O'Reilly, handing out small brown paper bags to the kids who were grasshoppers. "These are your stomachs. When I blow my whistle, you grasshoppers will have sixty seconds to collect your breakfast and put it in your bag."

Charu's hand shot up. "What do we eat?"

"This." Ms. O'Reilly walked around sprinkling little scraps of paper on the grass. She blew her whistle.

Charu, Lisbet, Mariah, Ben B. and Ben T., and all the other grasshopper kids started running around like crazy, snatching bits of paper and putting them in the bags. Everyone was shrieking and laughing and having a good time.

Everyone except Josh. His frog might be *dying*. And every time he tried to talk to his teacher, she ignored him. What was the point of raising your hand and asking for permission anyway?

"Ms. O'Reilly," he said quickly, "can I go get my frog? 'Cause it's really warm out here and maybe it would like that. Maybe it needs fresh air. I could put it in that bucket and bring it outside, okay? 'Cause I think there's something wrong with it."

Ms. O'Reilly didn't answer. She blew her whistle and called, "Stop! No more eating, grasshoppers. Hold onto your paper bags." Turning to Josh, she said, "I wish you had thought of that before we came out here, Joshua. I don't want to interrupt our activity."

"I *tried* asking!" protested Josh. "And you said, 'Not now'!"

Pointing out that he was right and she was wrong didn't win Josh anything. Ms. O'Reilly ignored him and shouted instructions. "Time for part two: the frogs are looking for their breakfast. Now remember, this is tag, not tackle. There will be severe consequences for any frog tackling a grasshopper!"

Josh tried again. "I can run up right now and you can keep going."

"No, Josh, not in the middle of our activity," she said, and blew her whistle. Kids started yelling and running. The three frog kids were chasing and tagging out the grasshopper kids.

"Can I go *now*?" pleaded Josh. "I promise I'll be really really quick!"

"It's not a good time, Josh," she said, "because now the hawk is looking for breakfast!" Turning away from Josh, she split the air with a screeching whistle.

Josh was standing so close he thought his eardrum might split, too.

"Josh, go!" shrieked Charu. "It's your turn!"

Josh looked around. Michael, Payson, and Kendra—the three frog kids—were watching him warily, ready to run. The grasshopper kids were watching. They all wanted him to chase the frogs. Nobody cared that the real frog was back in the classroom, all alone.

Payson came hopping over. "Come on," he said. "Try and catch me!"

"No," said Josh. What was the point of doing an activity on the food chain when his frog might need actual food? "I'm not running."

Payson gave Josh a look. "Ms. O'Reilly," he called. "What should I do?"

"Josh," said Ms. O'Reilly. "What's the problem?"

"I *told* you what the problem was," said Josh. "And you don't even care!"

Payson fell silent. The other kids stood nearby, not knowing what to do.

"*Nobody* cares," Josh went on. "They think it's weird or gross, but they don't actually care. They just make jokes and call it names and bother it by knocking on the glass. The only thing they care about is getting to go outside instead of being locked up in the classroom like my frog is locked up in that terrarium!"

The entire fifth grade was listening as Josh added, in a dead-on imitation, "And every time I try to tell you, you say, *Not now! Not now!*"

Ms. O'Reilly took Josh by the arm and led him a few feet away from the group. She was squeezing his elbow, and she had a look on her face like when his mom was squeezing the lid of a jar she couldn't get open. Mad.

"Joshua," she said. "I know how excited you are about your frog. But I still expect you to participate in our activities. Do you think you can manage that?"

"No," said Josh, "because—"

Ms. O'Reilly held up her hand to stop him. "I'm not listening to any more of this, Joshua. I want you to go inside and report to the principal."

Josh felt a blast of heat rush to his face.

Breaking the silence, somebody giggled. Josh turned away—quickly, so they couldn't see his face anymore—and started to walk—slowly, because even if Ms. O'Reilly could send him to the principal, she still wasn't the boss of him—toward the building.

Chapter 5

Gorman & Gorfman

The office was command central of Hollison Elementary. The secretary's desk sat next to a big glass window that looked out into the main hallway and the front door. Behind her desk was the door to the principal's office—you had to get past Mrs. B. to see Mrs. Gorman, the principal. Filing cabinets lined one wall, and in a corner was a low, round kindergarten table with a basket of paper and crayons.

That was where Josh sat down to wait. He knew the drill.

"Hello, Joshua," said Mrs. B. "I'll let her know you're here."

Josh couldn't stand waiting and doing nothing. He rummaged through the crayon basket, looking for the right shade of green to draw the frog. Not olive green. Not lime. There—moss green. He grabbed a black crayon for the spots and started doodling.

Last night he had read the entire *Big Book of Amphibians* he'd gotten from the school library. It told how a female leopard frog could lay thousands of eggs in the water, and then a male frog fertilized them. Then their job as parents was done. Mission accomplished.

Except *parents* was the wrong word. A frog didn't have parents the way people did.

Josh finished drawing the frog's body and started drawing the legs. He knew for a fact that his mom had never been sent to the principal's office when she was a kid. She had told him. What about his dad? He highly doubted it.

What about his birth dad?

Even though it wasn't a big secret about Jonathan being his birth dad, Josh still felt like he didn't know that much about him. He knew from the photo album that Jonathan had reddish-brown hair and green eyes, just like him. He knew he'd been a landscaper, and that he went fly-fishing in the summer and ice fishing in the winter. But he didn't know what his first dad was really *like*. It wasn't as if people went around talking about somebody who was dead.

Josh figured that asking his mom about the guy she'd divorced would make her mad, and asking Matt and Lacey about their son who died might make them sad. He was against giving his mom another reason to be mad at him, and he definitely didn't want to make the bio-grands sad. Which meant that he knew some basic facts, but not the important stuff, like whether his first dad ever got sent to the principal's. Like him.

The door to the principal's office swung open. Quickly Josh crumpled up his drawing and tossed it in the wastebasket.

"Joshua Tree Hewitt," said Principal Gorman.

She was wearing a navy blue dress with gold stripes and gold buttons, like some kind of captain's uniform, and she had a look on her face as if whatever she'd eaten for breakfast wasn't agreeing with her.

"I have a meeting in ten minutes, so why don't you tell me why you're here," she said, ushering him into her office and pointing to a chair. "And Josh— try to come right to the point, okay?"

"Well," he began. "I found a frog with three back legs! And Ms. O'Reilly said we could try to study why it got that way. So she took us outside to do an activity on the food chain. And some kids were grasshoppers and some kids were frogs and I was supposed to be the hawk. And probably we were going to find out that if the grasshoppers eat something and then the frogs eat the grasshoppers and then the hawk eats the frogs, that whatever the grasshoppers ate can end up in the hawk. And if it was something bad, like pesticides, then that's bad for the hawk. Probably."

Principal Gorman was looking steadily at Josh with her lips pinched together. Josh wondered if a real captain on a real ship would do as little talking as Mrs. Gorman. She didn't even have to say anything and he knew exactly what her face meant: Explain.

"Well, we didn't really get to the end," said Josh. "At least I didn't. 'Cause Ms. O'Reilly told me to come see you."

Mrs. Gorman lifted her eyebrows: Explain.

Josh knew he was almost out of time. And he wanted the principal to get it. Because this really mattered. He started talking as fast as he could.

"It was nice of Ms. O'Reilly to let us play that game, but I didn't want to make believe I was a hawk so I could learn about the food chain. I already get it! Pesticides—bad! But there isn't time to play games. My frog is sick and it needs help *now* and—I mean—isn't there some way we could get someone to come look at it?"

Mrs. Gorman checked her watch. "Joshua," she said. "Your frog sounds absolutely fascinating. But since it's Friday, I suggest that you bring it home and see if your parents can help you. I also suggest that in future, you cooperate with Ms. O'Reilly. For not cooperating today, I'm going to take away your recess. When your class goes outside, report back to the office."

Josh started to say, "But Mrs. Gorman!" but the principal held up her hand.

"Every time you speak, you will lose another recess. End of story." She pointed to the door. "You're free to go."

Josh headed back to fifth grade. How could he make her understand if he wasn't allowed to talk?

And what was "free to go" supposed to mean? He still had to go back to his class, and report to the office for recess, and get through an entire day inside Hollison Elementary. What was "free" about that?

"What'd Mrs. Gorman say?" asked Michael as the bus pulled out of the circle and headed down Route 27.

"I lost recess," answered Josh.

It had been a long afternoon, but finally it was over and Josh was riding home with Michael in the best seat on the bus—the last row. Josh had the bucket wedged between his feet so it wouldn't tip over. The frog sat in an inch of water in the bottom of the bucket.

"I heard in middle school they have two buses," said Michael. "An early one and a late one. So they can give you detention and make you stay after school. But they can't do that in elementary."

"So all they do is take away recess," grumbled Josh.

The bus lumbered on, dropping kids along the way.

"What about Silent Lunch?" asked Michael.

Silent Lunch was when the lunch ladies decided the cafeteria was too noisy. Then everyone had to be quiet. Or else you lost recess. Not just the noisy kids, but everybody, because they were supposed to be learning about community.

"Ooh," said Josh. "Now that's a severe consequence!"

The bus slowed and dropped a couple kids, then picked up speed again.

Michael pointed to the frog. "Does he have a name?"

Josh shook his head. "No. Not yet."

"How about 'Severe Consequences'?"

Josh laughed. He thought about all the phrases the teachers used. "How about 'Quality Work'?"

"'Best Effort'!"

"'Involved Citizen'!"

Michael giggled. "How about Gorman?"

"No way! What if she found out?"

"What could she do besides take away recess?"

"That's true," said Josh. He turned the word *Gorman* over in his mind. Gorman the frog. It wasn't quite right. "Hey," he said. "G-O-R are the last three letters of *frog*, spelled backwards."

"So?"

"So one more letter makes it spell *frog* backwards. G-O-R-*F*."

"Gorfman!" said Michael excitedly.

"Gorfman!" echoed Josh. "His name is Gorfman."

Michael grinned. "Gorfman the frog."

"Gorfman *T.* Frog," said Josh. "Middle initial T."

The bus slowed again and came to a stop. Time to get off. A few rows ahead, Cady stood up. Josh and Michael stood, too, and Michael started down the aisle behind Cady. Josh was having a harder time because everybody wanted to see the frog one last time. They were standing up in their seats and pushing into the aisle to get a better look as he went by.

"Let me see!" squealed Charu, peering into the bucket so that her braid practically smothered the poor frog.

"Hey!" said Josh, pushing past her, but then Diego, a fourth grader, stuck his hand into the bucket.

"I touched it!" he crowed, and turning to his seat-mate, demanded, "You owe me a dollar."

Josh had the feeling you got when you tried to put on a too-small shirt and your head got stuck and you couldn't see and you couldn't breathe and you wanted to scream *Get me out of here!* He had to get himself and Gorfman off the bus, fast. He tried to move down the aisle, but Payson stood up and blocked the way.

"Let me hold Freaky Froggy," said Payson. "Come on, Josh."

How could he have ever imagined that he and Payson were going to be best friends again this year?

He didn't want to be any kind of friend with Payson anymore.

"No," said Josh, but it was too late.

Payson reached into the bucket, held up the frog, and yelled, "Freaky froggy alert!"

"Put it back!" said Josh. He felt his face growing hot.

"Whoa," said Payson. "He's getting the balloon face again. Watch out, he's about to pop!"

"You better put it back!" shouted Josh.

Somebody cried encouragingly, "Fight!"

The bus driver roared, "Everybody sit *down* or this bus-cam is going straight to the superintendent!"

Josh stumbled through the next few moments—Payson putting back the frog, kids sitting down, him following Cady and Michael up the aisle and down the steps. The doors pulled shut and the bus chugged away.

"Wow," said Michael. "You okay?"

"Saved by the bus driver," groaned Josh. "How humiliating."

Chapter 6

Free to Go

Josh headed toward the backyard with Michael following, and knelt down beside the patio pool. Gently, he tilted the bucket.

The frog slid into the pool and bobbed up and down like a buoy as the water sloshed back and forth. For a minute it dangled there, head barely above the surface.

After what felt like an hour, Gorfman gave a kick and glided across the pool. Reaching a rock, it clambered on, half in and half out of the water.

"Go on, Gorfman," murmured Josh. "You're free now. You can go."

But Gorfman wasn't going anywhere. His throat pulsed and his eyes blinked. That was all. A hawk flew overhead and made a ring around the sky, then veered off over the woods at the edge of the yard.

"Come on," Josh said to Michael. "I'll show you something."

Josh kicked off his sneakers and peeled off his socks. So did Michael. Bare feet felt good. Honeybees were out roaming the yard, so Josh was careful to sidestep any dandelions that buzzed.

At the edge of the lawn the warm, springy grass started to feel cool and soggy. Then squishy.

Josh climbed over an old falling-down stone wall that marked the end of where he had to mow and the beginning of the woods.

Michael followed. "This is awesome," he said approvingly.

After a few minutes of bushwhacking through stands of saplings and ferns, Josh pointed to a clump of skunk cabbages. "Check it out," he said. "It's a vernal pool. It's here every spring and then it dries up."

"Awesome," said Michael again. "You think Gorfman came from here?"

"Maybe last year he did. Then he hibernated for the winter." Josh started to say, "But maybe there's—" when he and Michael both spotted them.

"Tadpoles!" they shouted at the same time.

Josh and Michael spent the rest of the afternoon catching and releasing tadpoles. They got totally soaked but they didn't care. They scooped up tadpoles as small as Josh's thumbnail and as big as his thumb. Josh talked nonstop, and Michael didn't mind. Josh was surprised that Michael talked nonstop, too.

"Think they're the same species as Gorfman?" asked Michael.

"Could be," answered Josh. He dipped his cupped hands into the water and pulled up a tadpole. "They could even be his descendants!"

"What if they're deformed?" said Michael, wading in deeper. "What if Gorfman had some kind of disease and he gave it to them?" He sounded worried.

Josh lowered his hands until they filled with water and the tadpole slipped out and wriggled away. "I wish we knew if Gorfman was messed up from the beginning—like, doomed—or if he started out okay and then something went wrong."

"Something like what?" asked Michael.

Josh was standing knee-deep in the middle of the pool. "Like . . . there was something in the water?"

"Like I'm outta here!" said Michael.

They were both laughing, but they came out of the water, flopped down on the ground, and talked about what to do next.

Maybe they should rescue the tadpoles. They could catch them and put them in the patio pool. But they didn't know if the water in the vernal pool was good or bad. They didn't know if the water in the patio pool was good or bad, either. They didn't even know if water had anything to do with what went wrong with Gorfman.

Josh and Michael hung out by the vernal pool all afternoon, until the peepers were starting their end-of-the-day peepfest and it was time for Michael to go home.

Josh led the way back through the woods. They stopped at the patio so Michael could say goodbye to Gorfman.

Gorfman was still sitting on the rock, same as

before. The peepers were peeping away. The sun hadn't set, but its warmth was all gone, like a bath you'd sat in too long.

Michael said, "Bye, Gorfman," to the frog, and he asked Josh, "What are you going to do with him now?"

Josh surveyed the grassy lawn, then the edge of the yard, out toward the place where the skunk cabbages grew. Where the tadpoles were. In the house, someone switched on a light, which made the woods seem even darker.

Part of Josh was curious. He wanted to put Gorfman back in the bucket so he'd for sure be there tomorrow.

Another part of Josh felt guilty. Gorfman looked worse than when he'd first found him. Maybe the terrarium hadn't been a good place for him. The guilty part of Josh wanted to take Gorfman into the woods and release him in the vernal pool.

But which was the right home for Gorfman? Where would he want to live?

It was too big a decision for Josh to make. "I think

I'll just leave him where I found him," he answered.

If Gorfman wanted—if he was even able—then he was free to go.

"Josh!" Josh's mom was calling. "Joshua!" her voice came up the stairs. "Are you up?"

Josh forced his eyes open. He definitely needed more sleep. But if he missed the bus again . . .

His mother shouted, "Joshua Tree Hewitt, you have a game in forty-five minutes!"

Game?

The game! That meant there wasn't a bus to miss! It wasn't a school day. It was Saturday and he had a game! He rehearsed the hit he was going to make. *Thwack—zoom—yes!*

No—

Wait a minute—

First he had to check on Gorfman.

Josh scrambled out of bed and ran downstairs. In the kitchen Cady was eating breakfast, and his mom was packing rice cakes and water bottles into a canvas bag.

"Where's your uniform?" asked his mother.

"Just a sec!" Josh called without stopping. He banged through the back door and down the porch steps.

There was Gorfman! He was still there! He was swimming in the water! Josh's heart gave a little jump inside him, and so did Josh, leaping to the patio.

Then his heart took a dive. Gorfman wasn't swimming. He was floating, belly-up. Gorfman was still there because he was dead.

Chapter 7

Suspended

Wading into the water, Josh picked up the frog and sat down at the edge of the pool. The frog felt limp and heavy in the palms of his hands, and the legs didn't fight to get away anymore. They just hung down. The skin was cold.

Josh felt sick. His insides felt the way the frog *looked*—all heavy and limp.

Josh's mom stood at the back door. "Josh, honey, time to go," she called.

Josh looked up. "What?"

"Time to *go*," she said. "Your game starts in half an hour. I made you an egg sandwich to eat in the car, but if you don't hustle and get dressed you'll be late."

"Mom," said Josh. "He's dead."

His mom made a funny, wrinkled-up face and hurried over. "Oh, honey," she said. "No!" She sat down beside Josh, put her arm around his shoulder, and squeezed him toward her.

His mom's hug made Josh feel funny, as if he might—he didn't know—cry or something. He shrugged his shoulders to make her arm slide off him.

"Do you want to skip the game today?"

"I can't!" he cried. "You can't just not show up!"

"We can explain to your coach that you weren't feeling well."

"But I'm not sick! It's not like I threw up or have a fever or something."

"That doesn't mean you're feeling up to playing."

"I can't just not show up!" he shouted. "What about being on a team? Not letting down your teammates! I have to go! What about all your lectures on *commitments*?"

"You don't *have* to go," she said. "But you do have to make up your mind instead of turning this into an argument with me. If you're going, get dressed and get in the car!" She stood up, took a deep breath, and said in a calmer voice, "You have five minutes to decide."

Josh hated it when grown-ups pretended you had a choice when you really didn't.

He went inside, ran upstairs, and tugged on his uniform, then ran out to where the whole family was waiting in the car.

His dad started the engine, and his mom thrust a tinfoil package at him.

Josh unwrapped the foil, and the smell of cooked egg steamed up. He took a bite, chewed, and swallowed. But it didn't exactly feel right. His stomach was saying: no food allowed. Josh wrapped the sandwich back up.

Cady looked up from her book—this one had a white horse on the cover—and said, "Sorry about your frog."

"Thanks," Josh muttered.

"Cady," said their father, "don't bother your brother."

"What," protested Cady. "Should I just pretend nothing happened?"

"Maybe he doesn't want to talk about it," said their mother.

His mom and dad started lecturing Cady about not invading people's privacy. Usually Josh would have been happy that Cady was getting in trouble instead of him. But he couldn't feel happy about anything right now. He just had that no-food-allowed feeling in his stomach. He looked out the window as they sped past the gas station, then the field full of wild lupines, then the school, and then they were pulling into the parking lot of the Hollison Parks and Rec fields.

"Later!" said Cady, scrambling from the car and running toward the playground.

"Later," echoed Josh. He got out and headed toward his team. Everyone was there—Payson and the two Bens and some homeschool kids and Cameron, the coach's kid. Cameron was only nine, but he played on this team because his dad had been drilling the kid since he could walk.

Coach Bell was bald, and Josh could never stop the little ditty that sang in his head: *Bald Bell has the bat, bald Bell has the ball.*

Coach Bell scowled at Josh. "You're late." He was a stickler for punctuality.

Josh started to explain, but he didn't get any further than the word "I—" before the coach held up his hand.

"We don't have time for one of your explanations, Mr. Hewitt. These kids have already warmed up, so I guess you'd better do the same. Take two laps, please. Now."

Josh took off around the diamond. Coach Bell acted like he was just making him warm up, but Josh knew it was punishment. He wasn't stupid! He ran out to first base, then to second, then down the third base line, past the opposing team in their dugout. Some of the kids pointed at him. Now he rounded home and started down the first base line again.

Payson called out, "Hey, you might go faster if you had another leg!"

Josh stopped, panting. "What did you say?"

"You need another leg, like your freaky froggy." Payson laughed.

"That's not funny!" shouted Josh. "You can't make fun of my frog!"

"I'm just kidding!" said Payson. "You don't need to go all ballistic—I mean balloony!"

"Whoa!" said Cameron. "I think Josh looks a little upset!"

"I'm not upset!" said Josh, clenching his hands into balls.

"One more lap, Mr. Hewitt," called the coach.

"Ribbit!" said Payson, laughing. "Ribbit!"

Josh flew at Payson. "You can't say that!"

Big-and-solid Payson looked surprised, but not so surprised that he couldn't put up his arms to fend Josh off. They collided, and Josh started hitting and Payson started shoving.

Kids were shouting and Cameron called, "Dad! Dad!"

It was almost like he and Payson were just rough-and-tumbling, like they used to do. Except this time it counted.

Payson lunged and grabbed Josh's arm, and they both went down together. Josh slammed onto the hard dirt with Payson on top of him.

The fall knocked the wind out of Josh. It felt sort of like when you swallowed water. His lungs didn't work right and he couldn't catch his breath. And it *hurt*.

Payson was crushing him. Josh wanted to say "Get Off!" but he couldn't even breathe right, let alone talk. Josh had to get him off. He swung his arm and got Payson right in the face. Blood started oozing out of Payson's nose.

Josh felt a hand wrap around his wrist and drag him up from the ground.

"Mr. Hewitt," said Coach Bell, still holding Josh's wrist. "You are suspended from today's game."

Josh felt as if he'd just stepped off a roller coaster. Everything was a crazy blur. Bright red blood gushing out of Payson's nose. Bald Bell whipping out a white handkerchief. His mom and dad rushing over, each grabbing an arm, steering him away.

"I knew this was a bad idea," said his mother. "You were so upset about that frog. You should have just stayed home."

Josh opened his mouth to answer, but he was still working on breathing. All he could do was make a little squeaking noise.

"Hey," said his dad. "Maybe now we can talk without being interrupted."

"I don't think that's funny, David," said Josh's mom. Her face was sort of crumpled, like she was trying not to cry.

"Okay, okay. I know it hurts. But seriously, what are we doing here? What's the consequence for this behavior?"

"Maybe he shouldn't go tonight," said his mom.

"To Matt and Lacey's? Why's that?"

"Just because he wants to. Maybe you shouldn't get to give someone a bloody nose, and then go have a fun sleepover at your grandparents'."

Josh was pretty sure they wouldn't be talking like this if he was talking, too. It was weird. It was kind of like he wasn't even there. Just because he wasn't talking.

His dad shook his head. "I don't think so, Jilly. The coach has already suspended him from the game. Besides, that's not fair to Matt and Lacey."

Josh's mom shrugged. "I know."

"Please," Josh managed to squeak. Matt and Lacey had chickens and they let him watch television and everybody talked and interrupted each other and didn't get mad about it. "Please, can I still go tonight?"

His mom and dad looked at him. Looked at each other. Looked at him. Josh could practically see the gears moving in their brains.

He should be punished.

But Matt and Lacey shouldn't be.

But he should. But they shouldn't.

The way Josh saw it, his parents wanted to get rid of him, and Matt and Lacey wanted to see him, and he wanted to go. Everybody wanted it. But he could still see his mom hesitating, like it might be better to say no, and make everybody unhappy instead.

Cady came galloping up. "Mom," she panted. "Can I sleep over at Becca's tonight? Her mom said it was okay."

"So can I please go, Mom?" asked Josh.

He knew better than to ask for his own sake. He had to make it sound like it was for somebody—anybody—else. "You're always saying you and Dad should have some quality time where the kids aren't interrupting, and now you could have a date and you wouldn't even need to pay a babysitter!"

His dad shook his head, smiling. "Got your voice back, huh?"

"So is it okay?"

"Okay, okay," said his mom. "You can go. But you need to apologize to Payson *and* the coach, right now."

When you had a fight, grown-ups wanted you to make up. They wanted one kid to say "Sorry" and the other kid to say "Okay." Josh didn't understand why grown-ups didn't understand that that wasn't how kids made up. But he did know that if he didn't say the right thing right now, he couldn't go to Matt and Lacey's.

Josh looked over to where Coach Bell and Payson were sitting on a bench. Payson was holding a towel to his nose.

Last year they'd had a whole unit called "Working It Out!" with Ms. Kovich-Carey, the social worker. Josh had turned out to be really good at role-playing, so Ms. Kovich-Carey used to call on him to act out little skits, like inviting a friend over, or apologizing. Luckily Josh actually remembered the three parts to a good apology. Say you're sorry. Say what you did. Include the person's name.

Josh drew a big, bracing breath and walked over to where Payson was sitting. "Sorry I punched you, Payson. I shouldn't have done that. Sorry I was late and talked back, Coach Bell."

"Thank you, Josh," said Coach Bell. "What do you say, Payson?"

Payson didn't say anything.

Josh could feel the pressure building. He'd said

his line. Now all the grown-ups were waiting for Payson to do his part.

"Let's get this show on the road," said Coach Bell. "We've got a game to play. Shake hands, Payson."

Payson stuck out his hand and quickly Josh shook it. Josh wasn't really sorry and Payson wasn't really forgiving him. Why did grown-ups feel better if kids went through a whole make-believe making up? Josh didn't feel better. He felt gross.

Chapter 8

The Bio-Grands

He's here!" cried Lacey, squashing Josh in a big hug. She smelled like strawberries. She was wearing a matching pink sweatshirt and sweatpants, her usual outfit, even though Josh had never seen her running or working out. Matt got up from the computer. He was tall and thin, with reading glasses that perched on the tip of his nose. "Joshua Tree Hewitt," he said, taking off his glasses and tucking them in the pocket of his shirt. "Welcome!"

Josh slipped off his backpack and put a paper bag on top of the magazines that were piled all over the kitchen table. The television was on, but with no sound, because Matt was streaming in the baseball broadcast on the computer.

"What's in the bag?" asked Matt.

"My frog," said Josh.

"Matt, will you turn that sports racket down so we can hear?" said Lacey, shutting it off herself. "Josh, what do you mean you've got a frog in the bag?"

"It's not alive," said Josh. "It's dead. I want to bury it here, okay?"

"Absolutely," said Lacey. "We've got a special place for burying animals. Come on."

Josh and Matt followed Lacey outside. The bio-grands' yard was like their kitchen: messy in a fun way. There was a lawn mower, a wheelbarrow full of petunias in pots, and a blue tarp covering a pile of canned goods that Lacey was collecting for the church food bank. The chickens were out, scratching around the sunflower patch. This was where Josh had gotten his experiment seeds.

It was early in the evening, but still bright and warm.

Lacey took a deep breath. "Smell those lilacs," she said. "Smell those strawberries. I am pretty sure that heaven is going to be a June evening."

Matt rummaged through the toolshed and pulled out a spade. "I'll take a September afternoon," he said. "Apples and cider—and no mosquitoes," he added, slapping his neck. "Got 'im."

"Don't you think something might be done about the mosquitoes?" asked Lacey, taking the spade and starting to dig.

"Hold on!" cried Matt. "That's right where Shelby's buried! Push over a couple of feet." He pointed to a spot by some ferns where she should dig.

Lacey looked horrified. "I will not—that's where Jonathan buried all those hamsters."

Matt looked at Lacey like she was crazy. "What hamsters?"

"Don't you remember Luke?" demanded Lacey. "And Chewie? And Obi-something-or-other?"

Matt shook his head. "No."

"How could you not remember that?" Lacey turned to Josh, as if he alone understood what it meant to put up with Matt. "Your father had hamsters one year," she explained.

"I guess I'm having a senior moment," grumbled Matt. "But do you think we could discuss this later so Joshua doesn't have to stand there holding his dead frog any longer?"

"That's okay," said Josh. He kind of enjoyed listening to the bio-grands bicker. They were like a couple of squirrels, chattering and scolding, running up and down a tree. "I was wondering . . ."

The thing he wanted to know was how much he was like his birth dad, Jonathan. Josh was noisy and messy, and so were the bio-grands. He figured his first dad must have been, too. And his mom had left that dad. So where did that leave Josh?

He took a deep breath and asked the question. "Did my dad ever get sent to the principal's office?"

"Well," said Matt slowly. "I don't believe he did."

"Of course he did," contradicted Lacey. "It's only natural," she said to Josh. "I think it was something to do with his homework. Not always doing it."

"Why didn't I know this?" demanded Matt.

"Maybe you knew and forgot," said Lacey vaguely. "Or possibly I forgot to tell you." She winked at Josh. "Now where's a good spot?"

Josh grinned. Even though it wasn't exactly good news, he felt better, knowing a new fact about his birth dad: he had gotten in trouble at school, too.

"How about under there?" He pointed to a lilac.

"Looks good to me," said Matt.

"Wait!" cried Lacey. "I have to dowse for it." From beneath her pink sweatshirt she pulled out a small crystal on a chain and pulled it over her head. Dangling the chain, she let the crystal swing back and forth. Her eyes were closed.

Matt grinned at Josh and whispered, "First she's got to get her Yes and her No directions."

Josh nodded; he knew how Lacey did it. She couldn't ask, 'Where is a good place to bury the frog?' She could only ask, 'Is this a good place to bury a frog?' It was sort of like playing twenty questions—you could only ask something that could be answered with a Yes or a No.

Finally Lacey said, "It's good!" She handed Josh the shovel.

Josh didn't know if he believed in dowsing, but he believed in Lacey. He stepped on the shovel, and it slid into the soft ground. He leaned back on the handle and pried up a shovelful of dirt, and then another, and another. The chickens were making chicken noises, and Matt picked a wriggling worm from the turned-over earth and tossed it to them. Lacey was humming something that sounded like a hymn.

Finally he had a good-sized hole. He put down the shovel and took the frog out of the paper bag. It felt cold and heavy in his hands. The three big back legs dangled down.

Lacey made a sympathetic clucking sound, and Matt said, "You didn't tell us it was such a special frog."

"Most people just think it's gross," said Josh bitterly. "Or a big joke. They don't really care."

He set Gorfman down in the hole. The frog's eyes were wide open. It seemed like they were staring at Josh. Saying: *Don't you care about me, either?*

Matt picked up the shovel. "Want me to fill in the hole?"

"Wait a sec," said Josh, kneeling.

He did care about Gorfman.

Because he knew how it felt! He knew how it felt to have your parents look at you like you were from another planet—to have your teacher look at you like she wished you'd move to another planet—to have kids look at you and laugh!

He couldn't put Gorfman in a hole and forget about him. Never talk about him. Pretend he never existed.

If he did that, how would he ever find out what made Gorfman grow three back legs instead of two? To find that out, he probably needed evidence. He needed Gorfman. That was the big reason he couldn't bury him.

Then there were about a thousand other little reasons not to bury Gorfman. The tadpoles from the vernal pool in the woods. Gorfman's babies, maybe.

Josh reached down and picked up his frog. "I changed my mind."

Chapter 9

Confession Time

Sleepovers at the bio-grands' meant going out for breakfast on Sunday morning, and then church.

They called it church, but it wasn't like any other church Josh had ever heard of. The building was in the shape of a dome. And the stained-glass windows were big squares of bright colors, not pictures of people from a long time ago. Best of all, you could bring your pet anytime you wanted, not just for the Blessing of the Animals on St. Francis Day.

Josh slid into a pew and opened up the comic book Lacey had brought for him. Matt slipped him a lemon drop.

After a couple of songs a lady with a poodle on a leash came up to the microphone for the Prayers of the People. She asked everyone to pray for the sick, especially Betty Malone, undergoing treatment, and

Ray Burnham, scheduled for surgery. Please add your own prayers.

For my mother, a voice murmured nearby, and other voices chimed in. *For Emily. For Charlie.*

The lady asked everyone to pray for the dead, especially Marilyn Ashford, whose memorial service was to be held tomorrow and in whose loving memory the flowers on the altar were given. Please add your own prayers.

"For Josh's frog," Matt called out.

People were turning around to see who was praying for a frog. The prayer lady asked the congregation to join in a moment of silence. Everyone was quiet except for the poodle, who gave a little yip.

Lacey put her arm around Josh and gave him a quick squeeze. Josh liked the way she smelled—like maple syrup from their pancake breakfast. He liked the smell of the beeswax candles, too. The sun coming through the stained-glass windows made him feel like he was opening his eyes underwater.

Confession time. Matt and Lacey's church had the

kind of confession where everyone said it together, out loud. On either side of him the bio-grands were saying the words: *I confess that I have sinned . . . by what I have done and what I have left undone . . . I have not loved my neighbor as myself.*

Josh sucked harder on his lemon drop.

He probably should confess to punching Payson in the nose.

But why was Payson acting like such a jerk about the frog?

And why did God even let a frog with three back legs exist?

But maybe it wasn't God's fault, he thought, as the last sliver of lemon drop melted on his tongue.

But how could it not be, since God made everything?

But sometimes people took what God made and messed it up.

Except why did God *let* them mess it up?

By the end of the service Josh had more questions than ever and still no answers.

During the organ postlude, Lacey leaned over

and whispered, "Go ahead and get a snack—just don't knock over any little old ladies."

Josh hurried off to the room where they served coffee and cookies. He took a brownie and bit off a chocolaty chunk.

Across the room he could see Matt and Lacey talking to some old ladies and a couple of singers in their purple choir robes. Sometimes Josh thought it would be cool to sing in the kids' choir because you got to wear a long, black, Hogwarts kind of robe. He saw Matt nod and point at him. Lacey waved at him to come over.

"I need strength," murmured Josh, grabbing another brownie and heading over.

"I gave them the basics," explained Matt. "And they want to know more."

A lady in a wheelchair piped up, "Tell us about your frog!"

"Even though it's dead?" Josh asked.

"Yes, tell us all about it!" She pounded her wheelchair's arm to make her point. "I can't very well go mucking around in ponds and streams, now can I?"

No way out. You had to be nice to old ladies in wheelchairs.

"I guess not," admitted Josh.

"He's a leopard frog," he began. "I mean, he *was* a leopard frog. They're green with round or oval spots. And except for the extra leg, he seemed normal. His front legs were okay and his head was okay and his skin felt normal."

By now more people were gathering round. Moms with kids hanging onto their legs. Guys Josh had seen carrying up baskets of food during the service.

A lady in a straw hat asked, "How big was he?"

"Big," said Josh. "Like . . ." He searched for a good way to describe Gorfman's size. "Like three of those brownies! So I'm pretty sure he's at least a year old, not one of this year's frogs, 'cause they're still tadpoles. We found a whole bunch in the woods behind my house."

A little girl asked, "Are they his babies?" She was holding a doll with a matching blue dress and one of those giant toy horses just the right size for the doll.

"Well," Josh said uncertainly. He didn't know how much detail he should go into about frog reproduction with a little kid at his grandparents' church. "They could be."

The lady in the wheelchair said, "You remind me of my daughter when she was your age."

The girl with the doll and the horse asked, "You mean Mom?"

The old lady nodded. "Once your mother went into a great big muddy puddle and came out shrieking with delight. She had lost her sandal, but she didn't care because she'd caught an enormous bullfrog. They were brand-new sandals, too. And what good is one shoe without the other?" She laughed a tiny little-old-lady laugh.

"You never told me that story!" said the girl. "Did she get in trouble?"

"I don't remember," said the lady, shaking her head. "I just remember how happy she was."

"You must be proud of her now," said Lacey. "All grown up and teaching at the university."

"I have a question," said a man with snow-white hair and a purple choir robe. "How did the frog die?"

"I'm not sure," said Josh. "I never saw him eat anything. Maybe he starved to death. Or maybe . . ." He trailed off.

There was something he wanted to say. Something he maybe should have said at confession time.

"It's probably my fault. I shouldn't have taken him to school for sharing. Maybe it stressed him out too much. He spent a night in the terrarium and then I brought him home, and then he died."

For a minute there was silence. Through the open window came the sound of a car door slamming. The room was emptying out. The brownies were all gone and two ladies were washing coffee cups.

Matt put a hand on Josh's shoulder. "Time to go, friend."

"Goodbye, Grace," said Lacey to the little girl. "Goodbye, Mrs. Donatelli. Give our best to Dr. Donatelli."

"Will do," said the old lady. "It was a pleasure

meeting you, young man. And you mustn't think the frog's death was your fault. You did everything you could."

Josh didn't need a lecture from his dad to know that he shouldn't argue with little old ladies in wheelchairs, but he couldn't stop himself. "I didn't do *anything* for him," he said bitterly. "He's *dead*."

The lady held out her arm and drew the little girl toward her, "You didn't do anything *yet*," she said to Josh.

Chapter 10

Silent Lunch

Rain on Monday meant indoor recess. Josh was hanging out with Michael. The girls were reading or folding paper into cootie catchers, and the other guys were playing table soccer with balls of wadded paper or fighting with Payson to let them have a turn at the classroom's only computer.

Ms. O'Reilly had taken the telephone out into the hallway. She kept glancing in through the door's glass window, but as long as the noise level didn't rise so high it went through the door and interfered with her phone call, she stayed out in the hall.

"Hey"—Josh pointed at the picture Michael was drawing—"that's a good frog!"

"Thanks." Michael stopped drawing and sniffed the air. "What's that smell?"

"Popcorn," answered Josh. "Somebody's making

microwave popcorn in the teachers' lounge. Indoor recess is bad enough, and then we have to smell popcorn before lunch! There ought to be a rule against that."

"Not that smell," said Michael. "The candy smell. Somebody's got candy!"

Candy was against the rules.

"It's not candy," said Charu, pulling up a chair and sitting down with them. She jerked her head toward Lisbet. "It's excessive application of lip gloss. E-x-c-e-s-s-i-v-e. Excessive."

Lisbet had lip gloss in the shape of a Tootsie Roll. Every time she popped off the cap and smeared her lips the smell of Tootsie Roll filled the air.

"That's *disgusting*!" said Josh.

"I know," agreed Charu. "Spell that d-i-s-g-u-s-t-i-n-g."

"Did I miss something?" asked Michael. "Do we have a spelling test today?"

"Sorry," said Charu. "I'm working on my words. The middle-school spelling bee is in October."

"No offense, Charu," said Josh. "I know you're the

best speller in our class. But you'll be a sixth grader. Don't eighth graders usually win?"

"My mom says there's a first time for everything," said Charu. "My mom's way into me winning. Hey," she added, making a sorry-for-him face. "Too bad about your frog."

"Thanks," said Josh.

"How did you know?" asked Michael.

Charu shrugged. "Everybody knows."

"It was probably my sister," said Josh. Probably Cady had told every single kid she saw on the playground Saturday, and they had told all their brothers and sisters. By the time he'd gotten to Hollison Elementary Monday morning, the entire school seemed to know.

"So what happens now?" asked Charu. "Are we still going to study him?"

"I don't know," said Michael gloomily. "We spent the whole morning on math facts."

"You mean we wasted the whole morning!" said Josh. "We might not have much time!"

"What are you talking about?" asked Charu.

"Tadpoles!" said Josh. "In the woods behind my house. Pretty soon they're going to lose their tails and grow legs, and what if they grow too many? I need to learn all about deformed frogs, but I'm grounded from computer."

Payson shouted, "Score!" and pumped his fist in the air.

"Oh," said Josh. "Duh." He was sitting in the same room as a computer. All he had to do was get Payson off it.

Josh felt queasy, and not from the smell of Tootsie Roll lip gloss. He felt gross, remembering his phony apology and Payson's phony forgiveness. Yuck. Josh didn't want to be friends with Payson, but he didn't want to be enemies, either.

Charu marched over to the computer nook. "Time's up, Payson."

"Says who?"

"Says me," said Charu. "And I'm sure Ms. O'Reilly would, too, if I asked her."

Josh grinned at Charu. She was smart enough to know that Payson would cave, and she was right.

He moved aside and Josh took his place. Charu and Michael stood beside him, watching the screen.

"Thanks," said Josh.

"Whatever," said Payson.

Quickly Josh typed in "deformed frogs" and started moving through the links. He liked searching for information on the computer. It was like a treasure hunt.

Ben B. wandered over. "What's up?"

"What's up?" echoed Ben T.

"We're trying to find out what happened to Josh's frog!" said Michael.

"What happened to Josh's frog?" asked Ben B.

"It died, stupid," said Ben T.

"Bingo!" said Josh. "Check it out!"

On the screen was a frog that looked just like Gorfman, with three back legs. And another with only a single hind leg. And another with two legs in front and four in back.

"Cool!" said Ben B. and Ben T. in unison.

"What?" asked Kendra. She put down her book. "What's it say?"

Reading over his shoulder, Charu answered. "Some scientists think the problem is parasites."

"My little sister is a total parasite," said Ben B.

"Shut up," said Ben T. "I want to hear."

Charu went on. "There's a kind of parasite called trematodes."

"Like toads?" asked Ben B.

"Trema*todes*," said Charu. "T-r-e-m-a-t-o-d-e-s. They're some kind of tiny parasite that gets into the tadpole and messes up their development. Either the legs don't grow right or the tails don't fall off. Stuff like that."

"What else does it say?" asked Kendra.

Now almost the entire class was in the computer corner. Josh and Michael and Charu in front of the computer, the two Bens hovering behind them, and Kendra, Lisbet, and Mariah perched on desks. Even Payson had stuck around.

Josh scrolled down the screen to the next theory, and this time Michael read aloud. "Pesticides. It says there's a pesticide used to kill mosquitoes—"

The smell of Lisbet's Tootsie Roll lip gloss filled

the air. "We have tons of mosquitoes around here!" she said.

Everyone started talking at once. Josh was silently reading ahead as fast as he could.

It looked like scientists had tried testing tadpoles exposed to pesticides, and tadpoles exposed to trematodes. But they didn't always get deformed frogs. It didn't always happen with just one bad thing or the other bad thing. So then they exposed the tadpoles to both, and those were way more likely to turn into frogs like Gorfman. It looked like both bad things together were too much for the tadpoles. That's when they got messed up.

"So which is it?" asked Mariah. "Parasites or pesticides?"

"It's—" began Josh, when the bell rang to mark the end of recess, and Ms. O'Reilly opened the classroom door.

"It is far too noisy in here!" she said. "Everyone, line up for lunch. Except you, Joshua. I'd like a word."

"I'll miss lunch!" he protested as the fifth grade trooped from the room without him.

"This will only take a minute." Ms. O'Reilly slipped her glasses off her nose and let them dangle from the chain of sea glass. "I was sorry to hear about your frog, Josh. But we won't be studying it anymore."

"How come?" he protested. "Just because it's dead?"

"No," she said. "I don't want my fifth graders coasting for the next three weeks. I want you to be learning right up until the day school lets out. If we start now, we have enough time to squeeze in another history unit." She paused for effect, then announced, "Famous Mainers!"

"What famous Mainers?" cried Josh. "There aren't any!"

"That sort of misconception is exactly why we need to do this unit."

Josh tried to tell her what they had just discovered about parasites and pesticides, but Ms. O'Reilly held up her hand to silence him, while she went on about what a good idea this was. Finally she wrapped up her lecture.

"You better hurry if you don't want to miss lunch," she said. "And Josh, I really am sorry about your frog."

Stunned, Josh headed downstairs. In the cafeteria, the teacher aides who had lunch duty were patrolling with grim faces. On rainy days, when the kids hadn't gone outside for recess, lunch was extra zooey. Lunch duty after indoor recess was well known as the worst job in the school.

"Over here," called Michael, waving. He had saved Josh a seat.

Usually boys sat at one end of the fifth-grade table and at the other end sat the girls who only talked to girls. The middle was sort of a neutral zone, filled with kids who usually talked to nobody—Michael— or who could talk to anybody—Charu.

Josh dropped his tray on the table and squeezed in between Michael and Charu. That was normal. They were middle-of-the-table kids. What was weird was that Ben B. and Ben T. and Kendra were sitting across from him. The two Bens were definitely boys'-end kind of guys. And Kendra usually sat alone and read. Now she had her book open, but she wasn't looking at the page. She was looking at Josh.

"What did Ms. O'Reilly say?" she asked.

Josh picked up his sandwich and tossed it back down. He was too mad to eat. "She says we're not going to study amphibians anymore. She has something more important for us to study!"

"What?" asked Mariah, who was sitting next to Kendra.

From way down at the girls' end of the table, Lisbet, who didn't like to be left out of anything, called, "I can't hear!"

The noise in the cafeteria was so loud that Josh had to shout to be heard. *"Famous Mainers!"*

One of the lunch ladies, Mrs. Sturdevant, also known as Stoneface, walked by and gave Josh a warning look.

"Hey, Mrs. S.!" said Josh. He wasn't scared of the lunch ladies.

"That's ridiculous." Charu opened up her chocolate milk and stuck in a straw. "Deformed frogs are way more important. It's so obvious she's just punishing Josh."

"Totally," agreed Michael, and the two Bens and Kendra nodded.

Everyone knew that Ms. O'Reilly hated taking kids out of the classroom, and she had taken the whole class outside on Friday, and Josh had noncooperated. The result: end of unit.

"Besides," Ben B. objected, "there are no famous Mainers!"

"Duh!" agreed Ben T.

"That's what I said," said Josh.

"You said 'Duh' to Ms. O'Reilly?" cried Ben T.

"No! I said there weren't any famous Mainers."

"Famous *what*?" called Lisbet.

Josh looked around. Half the fifth grade class was looking at him. Waiting for him to keep talking. They actually *wanted* him to talk.

He said angrily, "I told her there weren't any famous Mainers, and she said that was stupid. She

said she has to get us ready for middle school, and if we don't know our local history we'll be sorry when they give us the big statewide test. She doesn't want to spend time studying frogs because they won't be on the test."

"Test?" Lisbet sounded like she was going to cry. "When? On what?"

Josh shouted, "The stupid test on stupid local history they give us in stupid middle school!"

That was as far as he got before Mrs. Sturdevant swooped over to the fifth-grade table and, skipping right over the usual warnings, went straight for the worst penalty there was: "SILENT LUNCH!"

The cafeteria hushed.

All you could hear now was biting and chewing and slobbering noises.

And grumbling.

And the low, murmured sound of the culprit's name, the reason why every kid in Hollison Elementary had to endure Silent Lunch: Josh . . . Joshua . . . Joshua Hewitt.

Chapter 11

Power Failure

It rained all afternoon and evening. By the time supper was over it sounded like the wind was throwing the rain against the windows. Josh's mom started washing dishes; his dad was scraping food out of serving bowls and into plastic containers. Josh and Cady took out their homework.

Josh looked at the numbers on the paper. Sixty-four divided by thirty-two. Eleven into one hundred and ninety-eight.

Josh stared dumbly at his worksheet, but he couldn't concentrate. He began making a list of everyone who was mad at him, and why.

Ms. O'Reilly: Ruining her food-chain activity by talking instead of running.

Principal Gorman: Ditto Ms. O'Reilly. Talking.

Coach Bell: Talking back and punching Payson.

Payson: Punching Payson.

Mrs. Sturdevant: Talking too loud in the cafeteria.

Two hundred kids in Hollison Elementary: Silent Lunch.

Mom and Dad: Breaking the cabinet glass, talking too much, punching Payson. And they'd be mad about the Silent Lunch, too, if they knew about it.

"Mom," said Cady. "What's seventeen plus seven?"

"That's easy!" snapped Josh.

"We'd be pretty worried if second-grade math wasn't easy for you in fifth grade," said Josh's dad, rummaging in the refrigerator for room to put the leftovers. "What are you working on?"

"Double-digit division," said Josh. "And I know addition is easy now. But how come they couldn't just wait and teach addition when it would be easy? Like in fifth grade?"

"What about division?" asked his dad.

"We could do that next year!"

His dad asked, "How could you really know how

easy it would be for you to learn addition in fifth grade, since you already learned it in second?"

"They should do an experiment," said Josh excitedly. "Like what if they took half the kids in Cady's class and taught them addition *now*, in second grade, and then waited and taught the other half in fifth grade? And see which kids learned it quicker? You know it'd be the older kids! Then with all the time they'd save, they could do something interesting."

"Recess!" suggested Cady.

"Double recess," agreed Josh, grinning at his sister. "Or what would be really cool was if you could have two of the exact same kid! Like one copy of Cady would learn addition in second grade, and one of her would learn it in fifth grade. Then see which one learns it easier. I bet it would take her about five minutes to learn seventeen plus seven in fifth grade."

"Interesting," said Josh's dad. "But I don't think we'll give you permission to clone Cady."

"No, clone me!" cried Cady. "Then I'd have an identical twin."

Josh started to explain, "Not really," but his mother interrupted.

"Hold it," she said. "This fascinating discussion about the best way to learn math is not helping Josh actually get his math homework done. Stop asking him questions, David. You know how he is."

Josh burst out, "*You know how he is.* Why don't you just come right out and say that you hate me?"

For a minute everything was quiet except for the sound of the rain on the roof and windows. His mom and dad looked at each other, and then his mom sat down beside Josh. "Just because I want you to do your homework doesn't mean that I hate you," she said. "How can you think such a thing?"

"Because whenever I try to say anything you say I shouldn't talk so much. Everybody does. I can't say *anything* without getting in trouble. If I try to tell you something, all you say is *Don't talk back. First obey and then we can talk. You know how he is.* I'm not nice and quiet like Cady and you and Dad. I'm like—"

Thunder boomed so loudly that Josh didn't finish his sentence. He didn't finish saying that he was like Matt and Lacey, the bio-grands. And probably like Jonathan, his birth dad.

"Wow!" shouted Cady as a flash of lightning followed the thunder.

Josh's mom put her hand on his arm. "I don't hate you," she said softly. "I never have and I never will. And I'm sorry you've been having such a hard time lately. Did something happen at school today?"

Was this some sort of trick question? Did she know about the Silent Lunch? Maybe the principal had called to complain. Or had Cady told? Josh glanced sharply at his sister, but she was making an I-don't-know face, and Josh figured she was innocent. Then his dad said, "Uh . . . Josh?"

He was standing beside the open freezer door and peering into a wrinkled paper bag.

Busted. Could this day get any worse?

"Why is there a dead frog in here?"

"Because I put it there?"

The wind threw more rain against the windows.

Josh's dad took a big trying-to-be-patient breath. "You know what I meant. Why are you keeping your frog in the freezer?"

Josh's mom said, "I thought you took it to Matt and Lacey's to bury."

"I decided not to. I might need it."

His mom had a strange look on her face, like Josh was talking in a language she couldn't understand. "Need it for . . .?"

"To show somebody."

"Didn't you show everybody at school already?"

"Not everybody," interrupted Cady. "Only the fifth graders got to see it. The kids in my class want to see it, too."

"They do?" asked Josh, surprised. "You didn't tell me that."

Cady nodded. "I told them about it during morning meeting."

Just then the lights flickered off and on, then off again. Then on. Then off.

Then nothing but darkness and silence, waiting to see if the lights would come on again. As long as nobody else was talking, Josh figured he might as well. "Mom, this is really important. There's like a hundred tadpoles in that pool in the woods, and they could all get messed up, too! But there's scientists trying to figure out whether it's pollution or parasites. Gorfman could be a valuable piece of scientific evidence."

"Gorfman?"

"It's frogman, backwards. Sort of."

"Never mind that," said Josh's mom. "Why can't you just take some pictures?"

"Could we finish this discussion later?" asked Josh's dad. "Like when the lights are back on? Where's the flashlight?"

Cady jumped up. "I know!" She started crashing around the kitchen in the dark.

"Pictures aren't the same," said Josh. "What if they need the body? You can't dissect a photograph."

"I'm all for science," said his mom. "But my refrigerator is not a laboratory. I don't want to come across dead animals when I'm looking for chicken broth. What's that dripping noise?"

"Rain?" suggested Josh, trying to be helpful. Because even though she didn't want the frog in the fridge, at least she was still talking to him. Usually once one of them came down on his talking, the other one closed ranks. But apparently telling her that he felt like she hated him was a good way to break through their defense.

"Mom," he pressed on. "I promise Gorfman won't be in the way."

"Enough with the frog, Josh," warned his dad.

"Found it!" sang Cady, turning on the flashlight.

"The ceiling!" shrieked Josh's mom.

Cady was aiming the flashlight straight up at the source of the dripping noise—rain leaking through the ceiling. A big brown stain was blooming where the drops were falling thickest. The whole ceiling was starting to sag.

Josh's parents sprang into action. His dad grabbed a hand drill from the everything-drawer, stood on a chair, and drilled a hole in the ceiling, and his mom held a pot up in the air to catch the water that came sluicing out. When the water finally slowed to a trickle, she set the pot on a chair underneath the leak to catch any last drips. Sitting down at the kitchen table, she let her head rest in her hands.

Josh's dad lit a candle. He put the drill on the table, next to the paper bag. "I almost forgot," he said, sighing. "What do we do with this?"

In the light of the flickering candle, Josh's mom lifted her head and held up her crossing-guard hands. "Well, it's not going back in a freezer that isn't working. A frozen frog is bad enough. A defrosted dead frog is going to stink."

Crossing-guard hands meant that this conversation was over. The leak in the ceiling had pushed his mom over the edge. Josh needed an idea. Fast. He grabbed the flashlight and shone it around the kitchen, searching for inspiration. He saw the answer.

"I'll put it in my lunchbox. It keeps stuff cold, right?" Opening the freezer, he grabbed an ice pack and put it, with Gorfman, into his lunchbox. "This will be like a miniature cooler. It'll be fine. It won't smell at all, Mom."

His mom was shaking her head, but she was smiling. She reached out and rumpled his hair. That meant yes!

"Thanks, Mom. You won't regret this."

Josh zipped up his lunchbox with Gorfman inside. The tadpoles weren't going to end up like Gorfman. Not if he could help it.

Chapter 12

Xandra Screams

When the bell rang for recess the next day, kids started scrambling from their desks. Hot-lunch kids got in line right away. Cold-lunch kids got their lunch-boxes out of their cubbies so they wouldn't have to come back up to the classroom between recess and lunch.

Some kids always got hot lunch. Some kids always brought lunch from home. And some kids, like Josh, did both. If it was hamburger or pizza, he bought hot lunch. If it was something gross, he carried. Today was chop suey, so Josh had brought a bagel.

He'd also brought Gorfman. The rain had stopped in the night and the wind died down, but there was still no power at their house. He couldn't put Gorf-man back in the freezer, and he wasn't a hundred percent sure that his mom wouldn't change her mind and get rid of him.

Grabbing his lunchbox, Josh went to the end of the line and trooped downstairs. Outside, it was hot and sunny, as if yesterday's storm had never happened, except that kids were splashing through the puddles dotting the playground. Cady came running up with Becca and a bunch of kids from the lower grades.

"Becca wants to see Gorfman!"

"Yeah!" agreed Becca. "Can I see him?"

"Me, too," said a girl named Trina.

"Me, too," said a third grader Josh didn't know, who had a buzz cut and sticky-out ears.

"Okay, okay," agreed Josh. "Take it easy." He led the way to a puny little maple tree that was trying to grow in the middle of the big grassy area, sat down, and opened up his lunchbox. Cady, Becca, Trina, the buzz cut kid, and a bunch of other kids peered in.

"Cool!" said Becca.

"Ooh," cooed Trina. "Poor thing!"

Some kids stayed, staring, like they couldn't get

enough. Others ran off and came back holding the hands of their little brothers and sisters. Then those kids left and came back with their friends. Josh lost track of how many kids came to see Gorfman. Fifteen, twenty, twenty-five?

"Let me see!"

"I can't see!"

"Don't push!" said Josh. "Everyone will get a turn."

The kid with the buzz cut couldn't get enough. When Josh shooed kids away, the kid got back in line for another turn.

"What's your name?" asked Josh the next time the kid got to the front again.

"Kyle," he said. "I'm gonna get my sister! Hold on!" He ran off across the playground.

While Josh waited for Kyle to come back, the bell rang. Kids began swarming inside for lunch. Josh waited as long as he could, but finally he zipped up his lunchbox and went in, too.

Inside, Josh scoped out the fifth-grade table. He was so late that the only seats left were way down at the boys' end of the table. He slid onto the end of the bench, next to Ben B. and across from Ben T.

Payson was sitting beside Ben T. "Hey," he said to no one in particular.

"Hey," said Ben B. "Chop suey!" He made a mock karate chop.

"Sop chewey!" said Ben T., and laughed hysterically.

"That wasn't fair," said Ben B. to Josh. "Silent Lunch yesterday."

"Yeah!" agreed Ben T. "Mrs. Sturdevant was picking on you!"

"Thanks," said Josh.

"Watch out," warned Payson. "Here she comes!"

Mrs. Sturdevant came pacing between the long tables and paused at the boys' end of the fifth-grade table. Her face seemed like it was hardened into a permanent scowl, and even her hair seemed hard, like you wouldn't be able to get a brush through it.

"Don't talk!" said Payson. "Quick, eat!"

Josh took a big bite of his bagel, and Payson and

Ben B. and Ben T. all shoved food in their mouths. Just then Payson caught his eye.

And then he grinned. And it was like all of a sudden they were friends again. Josh started laughing, which wasn't great timing, since his mouth was full of bagel and cream cheese. He began coughing and choking and laughing all at once.

Mrs. Sturdevant stopped at their end of the table. "Mr. Hewitt," she said. "Are you all right?"

Josh swallowed, coughed, and nodded. "I'm okay," he gasped. "Sorry!"

Mrs. Sturdevant looked at him suspiciously, then moved on.

Josh and Payson and the two Bens burst out laughing.

Payson took half his sandwich and gestured to Josh. "I've got PB&J," he said. "Want to trade?"

Josh didn't really like peanut butter and jelly. But he did like the idea of not being in a fight with Payson anymore. And somehow, laughing at Mrs. Sturdevant together had felt like their fight was over.

Maybe offering to trade lunches was some kind of peace offering.

"Halves?" he asked.

"Sure," said Payson.

It felt like a truce. Not totally friends again, but not enemies, either.

They were swapping half lunches when somebody tugged at Josh's arm.

"Hey, Cady's brother!"

It was Kyle, with the littlest kindergartner Josh had ever seen. She had blond hair pulled back tight in two thin braids. She looked terrified.

"Hi, Kyle," said Josh. "I waited for you as long as I could."

"Xandra wants to see it," said Kyle.

"See what?" demanded Payson.

"The frog with the extra leg," said Kyle.

"You have the frog with you?" asked Payson. "I thought it was dead!" He looked half disgusted, half impressed.

"It is," said Josh. "It's frozen. I've got an ice pack."

"Kyle!" called Michael from the middle of the table. "You guys aren't supposed to be here! You better take Xandra back to the kindergarten table."

Now the entire fifth grade was watching Josh's end of the table. Xandra looked even more scared. Her blue eyes got extra big in her tiny-kid face.

Kyle didn't budge. "Show her the frog!"

Michael stood up and came down to the end of the table. "Kyle, go back! I know them," he explained to Josh. "Their mom's gonna freak if they get in trouble."

Josh hesitated. "I'll show her later, Kyle. Okay?"

"No," said Kyle. "Now."

"What should I do?" Josh asked Michael. "This kid's kind of stubborn."

"That's true," agreed Michael, frowning. "Maybe you should just hurry up and do what he wants."

Josh glanced around nervously. "All right, all right!" He opened his lunchbox and showed Xandra the frog.

Xandra screamed.

Xandra screamed the loudest scream Josh had ever heard.

Xandra kept on screaming, even after Mrs. Sturdevant swooped over and commanded, "SILENT LUNCH!"

A huge roar of protest went up from the fifth-grade table.

Payson jumped up and said right to Mrs. Sturdevant's face, "That is so unfair!"

Even right-answer Charu said the wrong thing: "Silent Lunch because of *one little kid*?"

Mrs. Sturdevant took Xandra, whose screams were subsiding to a whimper, over to the kindergarten table. By the time she got back to the fifth-grade table, Principal Gorman was on the scene.

"What's going on here, Mrs. Sturdevant?" asked the principal. She was wearing another outfit that made her look like she was playing captain dress-up, with a white jacket and big gold buttons. "And who is responsible?"

Mrs. Sturdevant pointed at Payson and said his crime, as if that was his new name. "Talking back," she said. "Talking back"—now she pointed at Charu— "out of his seat"—that was Michael. "And that one," she said, pointing at Josh, "he's got something in his lunchbox that made Alexandra scream."

"I didn't mean to!" said Josh. "I thought she wanted to see it! I wouldn't make anybody look that didn't want to! But lots of kids are interested in Gorf"—Josh tried to stop himself, but it was too late—"man," he finished.

"Interested in *what*?" asked Principal Gorman.

It was the silentest Silent Lunch Hollison Elementary had ever known. The entire school heard Josh's answer.

"Gorfman," he said. "It spells frogman, backwards—well, sort of. Actually the G-O-R-F does spell frog if you turn it around, but M-A-N isn't backwards, that's the man part—"

Usually Josh didn't even feel like he was talking too much, and then all of a sudden people were mad at him. This time he did know. He knew he should shut up, but it was like he couldn't stop.

"—I mean, I guess I could have changed it to N-A-M and had it be Gorfnam so the whole thing would be backwards, or actually I guess it would be Namgorf, wouldn't it?, but I didn't think of that. So"—he was finally managing to wind down—"it's Gorfman. . . . It's . . . my frog."

Stifled giggles began to sweep through the cafeteria.

Josh couldn't help himself. Giggling was contagious. He started to laugh, bit his lip to try and stop it, and ended up making a choked, chortling sound.

Leaning over, Principal Gorman slowly lifted the cover of the lunchbox.

Even Josh had to admit that Gorfman had seen better days. He was looking like . . . well, he looked like he'd been dead for three days, frozen, and then thawed.

Mrs. Gorman raised her voice so everybody could hear. "The students who were out of line with Mrs. Sturdevant will report to my office for recess tomorrow," she said. "That means Payson Campbell, Michael Robinson, and Charu Whitting. Josh, you will report to my office for recess for the rest of the week." Then, with a grimace, Mrs. Gorman began zipping up the lunchbox.

"Hey!" said Josh. "What are you doing with my frog?"

Gingerly, holding it away from her body, the principal picked up the lunchbox. "I am confiscating this."

As quickly as he could, Josh jumped up, but his legs got tangled in the long bench attached to the table, and he fell.

Nobody laughed. Nobody wanted to miss anything.

From the floor, he shouted, "You can't do that!"

"Actually, Josh," she said. "Yes. I can."

Chapter 13

Power Up

Josh headed straight for the vernal pool when he got off the bus.

"Wait up," said Cady, trotting along behind him. "Wait for me."

Josh climbed the stone wall. "Stop following me, Cady."

"I can come," she said, struggling over the wall and trotting to catch up. "You're not the boss of me."

"Look," said Josh. "I had a bad day, okay? Why can't you leave me alone?"

"You don't have to be so mean to me!" cried Cady. "It's not my fault! I didn't take your frog!"

Josh sighed. She was right. It wasn't her fault he was in trouble. That was the problem. It never was her fault. It was always his fault. Which made it really hard to be nice to her. Still, she had a look on her face Josh didn't like. That trembling-lip look he'd seen on Xandra's face just before she screamed. The last thing he needed was for Cady to start screaming or crying or run tattling to their mom about what happened in school today.

"Okay, you can come. But promise you won't tell Mom or Dad about Silent Lunch today." He thought for a second and added, "Or Silent Lunch yesterday."

"Deal," she said, sticking out her pinkie finger. She loved to pinkie-promise.

Josh wrapped his little finger around Cady's. "Come on," he said. "Follow me."

They bushwhacked through the woods. The ferns had unfurled even more since Josh had been there with Michael, but he and Cady waded through them easily. The bigger saplings he held aside for her.

When they reached the pool, Josh found that the tadpoles were all still tadpoles. No froglets yet. No way to tell—yet—if the tadpoles would develop the way they were supposed to, losing their tails and growing the right number of limbs.

Josh and Cady splashed around catching tadpoles until the water was too muddy to see clearly, then let the cloudy water settle and clear, then splashed around some more. A mourning dove hoo-hooed, and a chipmunk chit-chitted from a tree. Josh told Cady all about how amazing amphibians were: how tadpoles could get oxygen through gills, like a fish, but when they got to be frogs they breathed through lungs, like a human. Cady listened with a happy, important look on her face. She never told him he was talking too much.

They stayed out until they heard their mother calling, "Jo-osh! Cady!"

"Time to go," said Josh, and just to be nice, added, "Get your pony."

Back at the house, Cady galloped inside, the screen door banging behind her. A minute later she was back clutching two Popsicles in one hand and a toy horse in the other. She handed him a Popsicle. "Mom says it's all-you-can-eat-Popsicles 'cause the fridge is still off and they're going to melt!"

"Cool," said Josh. "Thanks."

The bucket he had used to take Gorfman to school was still sitting on the patio, and he grabbed it and scooped up a bucketful of water. "Power up, guys," he said, pouring water on the sunflower seedlings. "Make me proud."

"How can a flower make you *proud*?"

"It's my experiment," said Josh. "Lacey said the more I water them, the bigger they'll grow. I'm going to save the seeds from the tallest one and use them to grow more plants next summer, and then save the seeds from the tallest one again, and in a few summers I'll have the biggest sunflowers you ever saw."

"Like a new species?"

Josh sat down on the steps beside Cady and took an icy lick of grape Popsicle. "Maybe not a whole new species," he admitted. "But a new variety."

"If you make a new flower," she asked, "do you get to name it?"

"Absolutely," he said. "I mean, hopefully."

"What are you going to name it?"

It was Lacey who had given Josh the idea for his

experiment, when she handed him the seeds from her biggest sunflower, saying, "My best seeds for my best boy."

"I'm going to name it after Lacey," he said aloud. "Lacey's Mammoth Sunflower."

"You're lucky," said Cady. She bit off the last chunk of her Popsicle and started making her toy horse canter up and down the step.

"How come?"

She made her horse jump over his leg. "You have three grandmothers," she said.

Josh had always thought of Cady as the lucky one, not him. She had the regular number of parents and grandparents. She was the one who never got in trouble. But maybe she had a point. Matt and Lacey were awesome. Josh wouldn't want his mom and dad to know about the Silent Lunches, but he wouldn't mind telling Matt and Lacey. They would understand. Lacey had given him the sunflower seeds. Matt had said a prayer for Gorfman, right out loud, in church.

They wouldn't take the principal's side, like his parents would. They'd be on his side. They'd help him.

Wait a minute. Josh felt like his brain had just made a jump inside his head.

Matt and Lacey *would* help him. For real.

Josh ran into the house, grabbed his mom's cell phone, and punched in the number. When Matt picked up, he plunged right in.

"Matt—hi—it's me. Listen, remember that lady at church and that little girl? And the mom—I mean the little girl's mom and the old lady's daughter—liked frogs? And then how she ended up being a teacher? Do you think maybe she would want to see Gorfman?"

"My guess is she most definitely would," said Matt. "Seeing as she's a biologist."

"So could you maybe find out if—you know—I could talk to her?"

"I'm on it," said Matt. "I'll call Mrs. Donatelli right now and see if I can get Dr. Donatelli's phone number. I'll let you know as soon as I get in touch with her."

Josh snapped the phone shut and did a little dance.

"You're in a good mood," said his mom, coming into the kitchen. "Did you have a good day at school?"

"Not exactly," said Josh. "But it's getting better."

Chapter 14

Plan A

When Josh, Michael, Payson, and Charu reported to the office on Wednesday, the secretary used one hand to point out where they should sit, and with her other hand she picked up the phone: "Hollison Elementary, this is Mrs. Burton, how can I help you?"

Josh sat down in one of the kindergarten-size seats. Through the open window floated the shouts of the kids at recess, and a warm breeze that made Josh wish he was outside. He bet Michael and Payson and Charu wished they were outside, too.

Charu was silently fiddling with the end of her braid. "Did Mrs. Gorman call anybody's parents? She didn't call mine."

"No," said Michael. He took a piece of paper from

the basket in the middle of the table and started drawing.

"Me neither," said Payson, folding a piece of paper into a box and batting it across the table to Josh.

"She didn't call my house, either," said Josh in a low voice. "Which is good, 'cause I'm already grounded from computer for . . . something else."

"Maybe she was embarrassed," offered Michael, "because of the name thing. Gorfman. Gorman."

"No," Payson disagreed. "They only call home for big stuff. Like if you hit someone."

Payson sounded like he knew what he was talking about. Josh wondered who he had hit.

Josh flicked the paper box back to Payson, then pushed the basket of crayons toward Charu. "Here," he said. "You're allowed to draw."

"We are?" she whispered.

"Haven't you ever had office recess before?" asked Payson in a surprised voice.

At her desk, the secretary held her hand in the air and slowly lowered it: *Keep it down*. Meaning, they didn't have to be completely silent. They could talk quietly.

Charu shook her head. "I've never been sent to the principal's before." She pulled a folded-up piece of paper from her pocket and stared blankly at the page. "Besides, I should work on my spelling. I'm supposed to learn ten new words a day." Her voice sounded like she might be going to cry.

Even though Josh couldn't even remember the number of times he'd spent recess in the office, he knew what a big deal it would be to someone like Charu. She was easily the kid most likely to win the good citizenship award at fifth-grade graduation. Or she *had* been. He put down his crayon.

"Sorry, Charu," he said. "I didn't mean to get you in trouble."

"It's not your fault," she whispered. "Mrs. Sturdevant totally overreacted!"

"Totally," said Payson.

"Totally," echoed Michael, nodding in agreement.

"You mean . . . you guys aren't mad?" asked Josh.

Mrs. B. hung up the phone, and for a moment nobody said anything. Then the speech therapist came in for her mail and started chatting up the secretary.

Payson leaned forward. "Sure we're mad," he whispered. "At Mrs. Sturdevant and Mrs. Gorman!"

"This is so messed up," said Michael. "You made an amazing scientific discovery and instead of us studying it, we're being punished!"

Charu wadded up her spelling list and shoved it back in her pocket. "And I went back to that site and it said that leopard frogs are on a *Special Concern* list. That's like one step away from endangered!"

They all started talking at once, until Mrs. Burton said, "Keep it down, kids."

Josh felt like he would burst if he couldn't talk. But he felt good, too. Payson and Michael and Charu were on his side.

Payson was probably on his side because he liked being in a battle against the teacher and the principal.

Charu was on his side because she knew that some things were more important than next year's spelling bee, and the frog was one of them.

And Michael was on his side because they were friends now. Maybe even best friends.

"Listen," whispered Josh. "There are tadpoles that could end up deformed if we don't do something. I've got to get Gorfman back so I can show him to somebody who knows about all that parasite and pesticide stuff."

"Somebody like who?" asked Payson.

"I'm working on it," said Josh. "I heard about this biologist. She's a teacher at a college and she's way into frogs."

Michael nodded. "Cool."

"But first we've got to get Gorfman back," said Josh. "So—are you guys up for helping me?"

"Of course we are," said Charu. "But how are

you going to show that you know the meaning of *respect*?"

"And *responsibility*," added Michael, quickly scribbling something and then holding up his drawing for them to see. It was a frog with two heads. In a cartoon bubble, one head was saying, Respect. The other head was saying, Responsibility.

After Mrs. Gorman had confiscated the frog, she'd explained that she wouldn't destroy his property. But she would keep it until he could show her that he could be responsible and respectful of school rules.

"I wonder where she's keeping Gorfman," said Michael.

Charu said, "She has to keep him cold, right?"

"She better be!" said Josh.

"So where is there a refrigerator?" she asked.

Josh and Payson exchanged a you-thinking-what-I'm-thinking? look and shouted in unison, "Teachers' lounge!"

"Keep it down!" warned Mrs. B., training a severe

gaze on them for a full minute before turning back to her work.

Charu whispered, "Stealing Gorfman from the teachers' lounge is *not* going to show the principal that you know the meaning of respect."

"I don't care," said Josh angrily. "I want my frog back!" But he knew they weren't going anywhere with Mrs. B. in charge of command central.

Michael was scribbling. He showed them his picture: the two-headed Respect and Responsibility frog was now sitting on a lily pad. On another lily pad was Mrs. Sturdevant, and the words in her cartoon bubble said, SILENT LUNCH!

"Silent Lunch!" mimicked Payson.

"Stop joking around," scolded Charu. "This is serious."

Josh repeated Payson's words. "Silent Lunch." Something about Michael's funny drawing was giving him a funny idea. "That's it!" he said. "Silent Lunch!"

Charu sighed. "It's your frog! Don't you want to make a plan to get it back?"

"Silent Lunch!" he repeated in a low voice. "That *is* the plan. They're always asking us to keep the noise down, right? So what could be more respectful than everyone being quiet? We'll get all the kids to stop talking at the same time. It'll be our very own Silent Lunch!"

Payson looked excited. Charu looked doubtful. Michael looked excited *and* doubtful. But when Josh asked, "You guys with me?" they all nodded.

"All right then," said Josh in a satisfied whisper. "It's the Get-Gorfman-Back Silent Lunch. Tomorrow at noon. Be there."

Chapter 15

Plans B, C, D & E

Josh lay in bed, trying to think. *Think,* he commanded himself. How was he supposed to let the entire population of Hollison Elementary know about the Get-Gorfman-Back Silent Lunch between now and noon tomorrow? He knew Michael and Payson and Charu would try to spread the word during recess—he'd still be stuck in the office—but how many kids could they talk to? A kind-of-quiet lunch wasn't the same thing as *Silent Lunch.* It would only work if *everyone* went along, and that would take a miracle.

He heard steps on the stairs and tapping on his bedroom door.

"Lights out," said his mom, opening the door.

"Mom, what's the definition of a miracle?"

She came and perched on the edge of his bed. "The definition of a miracle? You."

"Mo-om," he groaned. "That is so corny."

"You didn't say non-corny miracles," she said. "And I mean it. Somebody once told me that having a baby was like getting to help make a miracle."

"Who?" he asked.

"Your birth dad," she said softly. "Jonathan. It was something he read somewhere."

"So—Mom," he started, then stopped. "What was he like?"

Josh's mom sighed. "That's an awfully big question. Is this one of those let's-talk-instead-of-going-to-sleep conversations?"

"You never want to talk," he complained.

"I do want to," she said. "But not when it's bedtime." She stood and turned off the light. "Another time, I promise. Lights out, now. Go to sleep."

Josh lay in the dark. Through his open bedroom window he could hear the peepers peeping. He could hear the sound of the television from downstairs, too, because the power was back on after the storm.

Wait a minute. Electric power meant he didn't need a miracle. All he needed was ten minutes on the computer. He could print up a flyer that would explain everything, give copies to every kid on the bus, and ask them to pass out their copies to the kids in their classes.

It was brilliant. It was worth taking the risk that he'd be caught when he was still grounded from computer *and* it was lights out.

Josh sat up, pushed back the covers, and crept to his doorway, listening. He heard the low murmur of television voices. Coast clear. Quietly, he tiptoed down the hall to the computer room.

The screen was asleep—just like he was supposed to be—and Josh jiggled the mouse and opened a new document.

He knew Michael and Charu and Payson and the other fifth graders were on his side, but what could he say to make the rest of the school want to help him?

Maybe he could point out how unfair it was that the principal took his frog. Most kids were against unfairness. He decided to start with some generalities on the topic.

Do other kids in your family get more stuff than you? Do grown-ups ever take stuff away from you for a reason that isn't your fault? Then they say that life isn't fair! If you agree that <u>it isn't fair that life isn't fair</u>, please help me.

Josh hesitated. What should he say next? He could explain how he'd brought the dead frog to school because he couldn't keep it in his fridge because the power was out . . . but that was getting way too complicated.

Time for a brain break. Josh switched over to Mail and heard the *swoosh* of a message coming in.

Dear Josh [the bio-grands always wrote just like it was a real, old-fashioned letter]:

I am sending you this note because you're probably asleep by now, but this news is too exciting to wait. I left a message for Dr. Donatelli and she just called back. She would definitely like to see Gorfman as soon as possible. I gave her

your phone number and she said she will call you
tomorrow.

Love,
Matt

Lifting his arms in victory, Josh opened his mouth wide to let out a silent scream: *Yes!* Finally, somebody who knew something wanted to see Gorfman!

Except—*duh*—he couldn't show Gorfman to Dr. Donatelli. He didn't have Gorfman. Principal Gorman did.

For a second Josh sat in the glow from the screen, his head spinning. Pumped up. Bummed out. What next?

Fear next.

Josh heard the sound of silence—the television being turned off. Then steps, and doors opening and closing. His parents moving around downstairs. They were coming!

Heart thumping, Josh closed everything down,

raced back to his room, and dove into bed. Plan B was a bust. Okay, Plan C: Get up early and finish his flyer in the morning. Tomorrow was Thursday, so his week of no computer would be up. No problem, right?

Problem.

Which became clear when Josh woke to his mom's voice.

"Josh, this is the third time I've called you! Get out of bed!"

There was no time to write or print anything. No time to even think about it. In a hurry, Josh dressed, grabbed his backpack and an apple to eat on the bus, and staggered into fifth grade after having only been up for about thirty minutes. So he was still half asleep when Ms. O'Reilly said, "Does anybody know where Mariah is? It's her turn to do morning announcements."

Lisbet answered, "She's coming late today. She had a doctor's appointment or something."

Josh's sleepy brain suddenly sprang wide awake.

He had just seen Plan D. The most unbelievably perfect opportunity he would ever have to tell two hundred kids about the Get-Gorfman-Back Silent Lunch. Should he try it?

"Michael!" he said. "Payson! Charu!" He made get-over-here circles with his hand.

Michael, Payson, and Charu gathered near Josh by the terrarium.

"Listen," he said. "We have ten seconds to ask everyone not to raise their hand when Ms. O'Reilly asks for volunteers."

"How come?" asked Payson.

"Because she hates me, right? And she won't pick me unless nobody else volunteers. And I have a special announcement to make . . ." He trailed off. He didn't want to jinx it by saying his idea out loud.

"The lunch?" gasped Charu.

Josh nodded. "Will you guys help?"

Michael's face lit up as he understood the idea. "Sure. But will you wish me Happy Birthday?"

"It's your birthday?" asked Payson.

"No," said Michael. "But what are they gonna do, take away his recess?"

"Stop joking around," said Charu impatiently. "We've got to hurry!"

They spread out around the classroom. Kids were straggling in from the playground, dumping backpacks on the floor, hanging up jackets, getting settled. It was the perfect noisy, chaotic moment to make Josh's request. He saw Payson talking to the two Bens, Charu talking to Kendra and Lisbet, and Michael talking to some other kids.

"All right," said Ms. O'Reilly. "I need a volunteer. Who wants to run to the office and do the morning announcements?"

Josh raised his hand.

Nobody else raised theirs.

Ms. O'Reilly looked around the fifth-grade classroom.

Josh tried to look innocent, which wasn't easy.

"Well," said Ms. O'Reilly, putting on her glasses with their sea-glass chain and peering at Josh. "Thank you, Josh. You can go right now."

Josh slipped out of fifth grade, jumped down the stairs two at a time—against the rules, but who cared compared to what he was about to do?—and sprinted to the office.

"Hi," he said to Mrs. B. His heart was pounding. Did he look guilty in advance? "I'm here to do the announcements?"

Mrs. B. pointed to the chair he should sit in, next to the intercom system, and handed him the sheet of paper with the announcements printed on it: Today was Thursday, June 8, Happy Birthday to Ben Thibodeau and Graciella Norton, hot lunch was pizza, and students should please check the lost and found box, which was full, to see if anything of theirs was in there.

Josh sat, waiting for the moment when Mrs. B. would flick on the intercom and give him the go-ahead nod. Command central was busy at this time of day. The band instructor came in to check on the bus for the field trip to a concert next week (which made Josh remember that his permission slip was in the bottom of his backpack, unsigned). The gym teacher stepped in, wearing her trademark sweat-suit and a whistle around her neck, and asked if she could have a word with Mrs. Gorman.

"She's in a district meeting at Town Hall," said the secretary. "She won't be in until later."

Think! Josh told himself. *Focus!* What was he going to say?

He tried to think about what he had started to write last night, about how life wasn't fair. He couldn't think.

He tried to figure out what he could say to convince everybody that they should be quiet to help him get Gorfman back. He couldn't figure it out.

Instead of thinking or figuring, Josh was remembering. He remembered sitting next to Matt and Lacey on Sunday. He remembered the prayers for the dead people. That's what he wanted the Silent Lunch to be like. He wanted it to be a moment of silence for Gorfman.

So now what? Time for Plan—who knew? Josh

had lost track of how many plans he'd gone through. There was no more time to plan, anyway, because Mrs. B. put a hand on his shoulder.

"Ready?" asked the secretary.

Nodding, he pulled the microphone toward him. He held the piece of paper in his hand, as if he was really going to read from it. His heart was pounding. He was just going to have to wing it, like when he said grace at supper. No problem, right? Winging it was his specialty.

The secretary turned the switch.

"Good morning and welcome to Hollison Elementary," he began. That was the usual opener. Then your name.

"I'm Josh Hewitt," he said. Still on script.

Josh paused and took a deep breath, like he would if he was going to try and touch the bottom of the pool at the deep end. This was it.

"And I want to say I'm sorry about the Silent Lunches we had this week. They were my fault. I found this frog with five legs, and I felt really sorry for him. And he died, and I felt really bad, and I ended up bringing the frog to the cafeteria, which I shouldn't've done. So I'm sorry."

Mrs. B. and the band instructor and the gym teacher were all staring at Josh with stunned looks on their faces. Luckily for Josh, they seemed to be frozen. Nobody moved or said anything. Nobody tried to stop him, so he hurried on.

"Anyway," said Josh. "Some kids and I are going to have a moment of silence for my frog at lunch today. And if anybody wants to be quiet with us, that would be great. So thanks a lot if you feel like it. And whether you feel like it not, I'm still really sorry."

Josh put down the microphone, and since Mrs. B. still seemed to be frozen, he turned off the intercom switch, too. He looked at the secretary, wondering what his punishment was going to be, but she just looked right back at him. Her eyes were shining.

"That was"—she paused—"that was really beautiful, Josh."

Chapter 16

Frogly Awesome

Josh spent the next three hours in a daze, waiting for the hammer to come down.

First the secretary didn't scold him. She just gave him a big, squishy hug and sent him back to his classroom.

Then Ms. O'Reilly didn't yell at him. She told him to take a seat for Silent Reading. What was going on? Could Ms. O'Reilly think that he'd asked—and been given—permission to make up his own announcement?

As Josh walked to his desk, he felt the eyes of the whole class following him. And he felt it: they were with him. They would go along with the moment of silence for Gorfman.

Then came Band. Band was optional for fourth and fifth graders. While kids were getting out their instruments, Josh realized that the fifth-grade clarinets were having whispered conversations with the fourth-grade clarinets. Fifth-grade flutes were talking to fourth-grade flutes. And the fifth-grade trumpets were working on the fourth-grade trumpets.

By the end of the period, the fourth-grade band kids were in. And since this year the school was experimenting with multiage classes, soon those kids could spread the word not only to the rest of the fourth grade but to the entire third grade, too.

After band, Ms. O'Reilly announced that it was time for kindergarten buddies. Josh was pretty sure that in addition to having a picture book read to them, every kindergartner was personally asked to go along with the moment of silence for Gorfman.

Trooping back from the kindergarten room, Josh's class passed Cady's second-grade class marching single file to Art. Cady gave him a thumbs-up. Did that mean . . . yes! More second graders were giving him the thumbs-up! Cady must have talked to them.

The daze was getting even dazier. Band kids, kindergarten buddies, Cady's class . . . were they all going to join in a moment of silence during lunch?

Time for recess. Josh grabbed his lunch—he'd brought a sandwich in a brown paper bag, because the principal still had his lunchbox with Gorfman in it—and headed down to the office.

Mrs. B. gave him the old you-sit-there nod. So Josh sat.

Still no hammer.

Half an hour to go. Josh was having trouble sitting still. Half of him was scared the Silent Lunch wouldn't happen. Half was sure it would. Half was just curious.

Whoa—too many halves. But that's how he *felt*. Like there was too much inside him. He couldn't keep quiet any longer.

"Mrs. B!" he blurted. "How's your dog?"

Mrs. B. smiled and shook her head. "Darlin'," she said. "You know I can't be chatting with you. Why don't you pick a book and settle down?"

Josh took a book from the pile without looking at what it was. There was no way he could concentrate on reading.

Fifteen minutes to go. He wondered if Principal Gorman was back yet from her meeting. If she was, did she know?

Luckily, Josh didn't have to wait long for the answer to that question. The principal walked in with her coat on.

"Hello, Joshua," she said.

Josh managed to squeak, "Hi!"

Mrs. B. handed the principal her phone messages on little slips of pink paper, and the principal disappeared inside her office.

She didn't know! And Mrs. B. hadn't told! Josh wished he could jump up and give Mrs. B. another squishy hug, but he stopped himself. He tapped his feet and squirmed in the tiny chair.

Ten minutes to go.

Five minutes.

Four.

Three, two, one.

Twelve o'clock. Josh got up and walked out of the office and toward the cafeteria.

He passed the kindergartners' tulips and daffodils and *"things that come up in the spring!"* pictures that had been up ever since April.

He passed the nurse's office with the little cot.

He passed the gym teacher's closet where she kept all the jump ropes and soccer balls.

Moving more and more slowly down the long hallway, Josh was having the weirdest feeling. It felt like he was underwater. The way it was hard to move, and you had to sort of push your limbs through the water. And the way when you dove under, suddenly all the above-water noises disappeared and it was totally quiet.

He came to the cafeteria door and stopped. It wasn't just him imagining a weird underwater feeling. Part of the feeling was real.

It was the silence.

The silence was real.

Kids were filing in, lining up with trays, finding seats—all in silence.

Josh bought his milk and then sat down at the fifth-grade table between the two Bens. Across the table, Michael grinned at him. So did Payson and

Charu. Josh grinned back. He took his sandwich out of his paper bag, but he was way too excited to eat. He felt more like he might lose his lunch before he even ate it. Because it was so amazing that two hundred kids were going along with his plan!

It was really happening.

It was the Gorfman Memorial Silent Lunch.

It was . . . a miracle?

Josh wasn't sure if a Silent Lunch really qualified as a miracle. But it seemed pretty miraculous to him.

Beside him, Ben B. tapped him on the shoulder. Then Ben T. tapped him on the other shoulder. They were both signaling for Josh to look behind him. Teachers didn't usually come to the cafeteria—they usually stayed in their rooms, recovering from the morning— but there in the doorway were a bunch of teachers. Josh spotted his old kindergarten teacher, the band instructor, the social worker, and Ms. O'Reilly.

The crowd of teachers made way for someone. Principal Gorman was coming through.

"Mrs. Sturdevant?" asked the principal. She

didn't raise her voice, but everyone could hear her because nobody else was talking. Nobody was even moving anymore. It was like someone had shouted *Freeze!* in freeze tag.

"This is the third Silent Lunch we've had this week. Who is responsible this time?"

Josh waited to hear his name, but Mrs. Sturdevant answered too softly for him to hear the answer. Then there was a long whispered conversation. Ms. O'Reilly joined in, and so did Ms. Kovich-Carey, the social worker.

Principal Gorman scanned the cafeteria. Her gaze fell on Josh. She marched toward the fifth-grade table.

Josh remembered when he had first picked up Gorfman, the way he could see the frog's pulse throbbing in his throat. Josh's heart was pounding so hard he was sure it must be showing in his throat, too.

"Joshua Tree Hewitt," said Principal Gorman. Her mouth was in a straight line—definitely not smiling, but not that mad, either. And her eyes weren't glaring. They were more curious. "Is it true that you asked the school to join you in a moment of silence for your frog?"

Josh panicked. He hadn't thought this far ahead. The Gorfman Memorial Silent Lunch was going so great. He didn't want to blow it now.

What if he talked too much—that was practically a guarantee—and made the principal mad all over again? What if he—gross—threw up?

He looked around for help. He made a *will-you-talk-to-her?* face at Michael, but Michael, grinning, just shook his head and pointed back at Josh. And there was Charu, smiling encouragingly. And Payson making *say something* bug eyes at him.

They were his friends. They trusted him.

Josh took a big breath. It was like he had pushed the pause button—big-time—and now it was time to push it again. Time to unfreeze everyone.

"Yes," he said. And he smiled what he hoped was a respectful, responsible smile.

"And how long is this moment of silence going to last?"

"I don't know?" Josh admitted.

So lame! he thought. But somehow his answer seemed to be the right answer. The principal smiled. "Well, I think you can call it a moment, don't you? Go ahead and announce that everyone can feel free to talk. Then come to my office before you get on the bus, so I can give you back your frog."

Josh was in shock. "You *will*?" he asked. "I mean, thanks, Mrs. Gorman!"

He stood up. His legs felt wobbly. He was about to explain that the Gorfman Memorial Silent Lunch was over and that Mrs. Gorman was going to give him back his frog, but he didn't get any further than "Thanks, everybody!" before his words were drowned out by the sound of two hundred kids cheering and clapping.

Principal Gorman didn't even try to stop the chaos. She let everybody keep clapping and hollering as she left the cafeteria.

Josh sat back down. He still felt shaky.

The fifth-grade table was going nuts.

"Can you believe it?" asked Payson. "You won! That was awesome!"

"Totally," said Ben B., and Ben T. echoed, "No, toadly! Toadly awesome!"

"Not toadly," said Michael, laughing. "Gorfman's a frog."

"It's frogly awesome," said Charu. "F-r-o-g-l-y *frogly*!"

Josh sat back down and picked up his sandwich, but he knew he was still way too excited to eat. "Definitely not edible," he said. "Anybody want my lunch?"

Chapter 17

Heaven

Josh decided he was going to have to side with Lacey in the bio-grands' debate over whether heaven would be more like a June evening or a September afternoon. Because it didn't get much better than this: a Saturday evening in June with a no-cloud blue sky. Warm but not hot. The air smelled like berries, probably because Josh had parked himself right in front of Lacey's strawberry-rhubarb pie.

Unlike the Gorfman Memorial Silent Lunch, where nobody talked and Josh hadn't been able to eat, today he could eat just fine. And everybody was talking. His mom and his dad and Matt and Lacey and Cady and Charu and Payson and Michael and the Donatellis.

They were all here for the Gorfman wake, which his mom had explained was something like a party you had when somebody died, to help you say goodbye. They were all here to say goodbye to Gorfman, because after supper Dr. Donatelli was taking him to her lab, along with the tadpoles she and Josh had collected that afternoon.

The jar of tadpoles stood in the middle of the picnic table surrounded by plates of lasagna and mashed potatoes and pie. Gorfman was in the freezer.

Polishing off his mashed potatoes and starting in on the pie, Josh listened in on the conversation at the grown-ups' end of the picnic table. His dad was telling the story. *Again.*

"So I pick up the phone and it's Josh's principal calling, and I'm thinking, *Uh-oh!* And she tells me that Josh organized the entire school into being completely silent in honor of Josh's frog! And then I hang up the phone and somebody is calling for Josh . . ." He paused and motioned for Dr. Donatelli to take over.

"That's where I was lucky enough to come in," said Dr. Donatelli. She had taken off her hip waders, and now she was wearing cutoff jeans shorts and a T-shirt that said I BRAKE FOR FROGS. "After Josh called

Matt, and Matt called my mother, and my mom called me—"

"And told her what a charming boy Josh was," interrupted Mrs. Donatelli from her wheelchair parked at the end of the picnic table.

Dr. Donatelli was going to send samples of the water to the state lab, and monitor the tadpoles' development, and study Gorfman. And she had promised Josh he could visit her at the university. Josh was thrilled, but he had more important things to think about.

"Can I have another piece of pie?" he asked.

Beaming at Josh, Lacey cut him a piece. "Of course you can, dear." Her dowsing crystal hung from a silver chain around her neck.

Josh bit into his second piece of strawberry-rhubarb pie. At the other end of the table Cady was showing Charu the cover of her book, the one with a girl holding a horse by a bridle. Both the girl and the horse had the same kind of braid.

"Like that?" asked Cady. "Can you do it like that?"

"A French braid?" asked Charu. "Sure!"

"Come on," said Cady, holding her hand out to little Grace Donatelli. "You want to come?"

The girls went and sat down by the pool where Josh had found Gorfman. Cady turned her back to Charu, and Charu started plaiting Cady's long brown hair into a French braid. Clutching her doll, Grace watched.

Payson and Michael got up from the picnic table, too.

"Hey, Hewitt," said Payson, putting on his baseball glove. "Wanna play?"

"No way. Too much pie," Josh explained, patting his stomach. "Use my glove," he offered to Michael.

Michael and Payson moved away from the table and started tossing a baseball back and forth.

"Josh," said his mom, "I'm sorry I said you couldn't keep your frog in the freezer. That night the ceiling leaked."

She put her arm across his shoulder, and Josh didn't shake it off.

"I know," he said. "That's okay."

"You know you could keep it there now, right?"

she asked. "You don't have to give Gorfman away if you don't want."

"Or you can still bury him," said Matt.

"No," said Josh. "This is better. It's not like he's *mine*—like a toy—like I need to keep him. I'd rather have him be with somebody who can figure out how he got an extra leg so maybe they can stop it! 'Cause it's not fair!" Josh could get mad all over again, remembering how it felt when people looked at you like you were a freak. They weren't looking at him that way now. But he still remembered. He was always going to remember Gorfman.

"Thank you, Josh," said Dr. Donatelli. "It will be an honor to study your frog. And you promised to come help me, right?"

"Absolutely," said Josh.

Josh's mom gave his shoulder a squeeze, then helped herself to some pie.

His dad cleared his throat and said, "We're proud of you, Josh." His voice sounded funny.

Mrs. Donatelli asked, "How on earth did you get the idea for a Silent Lunch?"

"We had a couple of Silent Lunches already this week," answered Josh quickly.

All the grown-ups were looking at him expectantly.

Josh decided this was a pause button situation. Quickly he took a bite of pie, and then chewed as slowly as possible.

Okay. It seemed to be working. He wasn't saying every single thing he was thinking. And he wasn't feeling like he was going to explode, either.

But should he tell them the whole story? About how he *had* to do a Silent Lunch to get Gorfman back after the other Silent Lunch where the principal had taken Gorfman away? His mom said that sometimes not telling the truth was the same thing as telling a lie.

But he hadn't lied. Yet.

But if he didn't change the subject he'd either have to tell the whole truth, which he didn't want to do, or lie, which he didn't want to do, either.

Josh decided to try steering the subject in a slightly different direction.

"And I remembered those moments of silence they have sometimes at church," he said. "So I sort of put those two things together."

Except for Mrs. Donatelli, whose eyes were drooping closed, everyone was smiling at him. Josh was so embarrassed he took another bite of pie.

Matt helped himself to a piece of pie. "This is a very nice wake," he said.

"We had a nice wake for Jonathan, remember?" asked Lacey.

"We had a great big party," said Matt, "and a lot of good stories."

Josh didn't remember. He'd been way too young to remember when his biological father died.

And from what Josh knew, his dad—the dad he knew, David—hadn't been around when his first dad—Jonathan—had died. So he didn't remember the wake, either.

Josh's dad stood up. "Think I'll get into that game of catch," he said. "You folks can reminisce." Going past Josh, he leaned down and said quietly, so only Josh could hear, "Nice job on the button." Then he clapped him on the back and ran off to join Michael and Payson.

Dr. Donatelli rose from the table, too. "Be right back," she said. "Nature calls." She disappeared into the house.

Mrs. Donatelli was sound asleep.

That left Josh with his mom and the bio-grands.

"What kind of stories?" Josh asked his grand-parents.

His mom said, "Well, Matt got up—"

"Wait a minute," Josh interrupted his mother. "You were there? But weren't you guys—you know?"

"Divorced," she said. "Yes. But he was still the father of my child."

Lacey reached across the picnic table, between the pie plate and the lasagna, and put her hand on Josh's mom's hand. "It was good of you to come."

"So, Matt got up," said Josh's mom. "And he starts to talk about how the acorn isn't supposed to fall far from the tree."

She stopped talking and started laughing, and Matt and Lacey joined in.

"What's so funny?" demanded Josh.

Matt explained. "You know that expression, don't you? It means that the acorn is going to grow up to be just like the oak tree it came from, right? The way children are like their parents?"

Josh nodded. "Yeah, I know that."

"Well, the joke was that Jonathan wasn't very much like me at all."

"Or me," offered Lacey.

Josh couldn't believe what he was hearing. "You mean . . . he didn't talk a lot? Like you guys?"

Matt and Lacey shook their heads. No.

Josh's mom said, "I guess it skipped a generation. You've got the gift of gab, like Matt and Lacey here. But Jonathan was a pretty quiet guy."

Josh's head was spinning. That meant that his mom *hadn't* split up with his first dad for being a motormouth. His birth dad wasn't just like him, and he wasn't just like his birth dad. He was like . . . himself. Which meant that when his entire family got mad at him they were just . . . mad at him. Which they were probably still going to get on a regular basis.

But right now nobody was mad.

His dad was hitting grounders to Michael and Payson.

Cady was brushing Charu's hair, and Grace was watching and clutching her doll.

Dr. Donatelli was back outside, leaning over her mother's wheelchair and saying something quietly to her mom.

And the bio-grands were bickering over whether apple was the king of pies (according to Matt) or whether it was strawberry-rhubarb (that was Lacey).

Josh's mom asked, "What do you think of this wake? Do you want to say a few words about your frog?"

"Wait a second," Josh said. He couldn't resist the chance to tease his mom. "Did I hear you right? *You're* asking *me* to talk?"

"Yes, Joshua Tree Hewitt," said his mom. "I'm asking."

"Ask me again," said Josh. "And say please."

His mom smiled. "Please," she said. "Now don't push your luck, Hewitt."

Josh grinned. "Can I make a toast?"

"Sure thing," she said. "Let me fill your glass."

"No, wait." He lifted up a forkful of strawberry-rhubarb pie. "Hey, everybody! It's a pie toast!"

His mom saluted with her fork, and so did Matt and Lacey. The others stopped what they were doing and gathered round the picnic table. His dad and Michael and Payson. Charu and Cady and Grace. Mrs. Donatelli and Dr. Donatelli. Everybody grabbed a fork and dug into the pie.

"In memory of Gorfman!" said Josh. "Gorfman T. Frog."